CLOVIS ACADEMY LEGACY
BOOK ONE

REIGN OF DEATH

By
Ross Harringway

CLOVIS ACADEMY LEGACY:

REIGN OF DEATH

OMEGA PRESS

An imprint of Omega Communications Group, Inc.

For information contact:

Omega Press
5823 N. Mesa, #839
El Paso, Texas 79912

FIRST EDITION

Printed in the United States of America

PROLOGUE

"I was known as Robert Richard Andrews. My closest friends and family affectionately called me RA. I am no longer among you. Before I faded away from the history of humanity, I dispatched dozens of communication canisters from my ship that had been named the Calypso. I was her last Captain. Most of the canisters were destroyed when they were drawn by the gravitational pull of the binary sun system of planet Akarzdamedia. Many are still floating aimlessly in space, waiting to be found by a passing space ship so that the truth of what happened to me and my crew may finally be revealed.

"I was an astro-physicist from planet Earth. Before the Akarzdamedians landed on Earth with their technologically advanced space craft, I had been assigned by the United Nations Science and Space Exploration Council to take command of the Calypso. My orders were to chart each of the moons orbiting Jupiter and to obtain samples of each of those satellites for closer inspection and examination. The Calypso was an older model science ship that had been slated to be turned into a museum for school age children to marvel over. The mission to Jupiter was to be her last. She could hold no more than fifty-eight crew members. I was graciously given the permission to select my crew.

"I brought in my best friend, astronaut Javier Perez-Guerrero, to act as the chief pilot and second in command of the mission. I selected my own daughters to serve in various sections of the ship. My youngest child, Judy Andrews, was my chief computer operative. Lorraine Andrews was assigned to work in the engineering section. Valeria Andrews was to head up our stellar cartography section. Elsa Andrews was an exceptional astronaut in her own right and assisted Javier. Janice Andrews was assigned to be our lead geologist. Jennifer Andrews served as our climatologist. Pamela Andrews was to serve as our medical doctor and monitor all life support systems on the ship. Elvia Andrews was brought on as another flight astronaut. The rest of the crew consisted of specially selected scientists and medical staff.

"We left Earth over two hundred years ago to complete our mission. That was just before all of the history of humanity changed direction with the arrival of the alien race called the Akarzdamedians. They landed on Earth with dozens of massive space craft and they claimed to want to have an understanding between our species, to collaborate and cooperate with us. We that had worked in the sciences were ecstatic at this contact with a new species. We were not the only intelligent life form in the cosmos. Although many humans were apprehensive or terrified, we celebrated. It was perhaps the greatest moment in the history of our existence.

"But the feeling of jubilation and elation did not last.

"Soon after the arrival of the aliens, the continent of Africa was hit by some weapons of unknown origin. At first, we believed that a few hundred million people died. Later it was calculated that a billion men, women and children perished in the attack. It was the worst disaster in the history of humanity. Africa had been the location for many of the United Nations long range offensive nuclear weapons silos. Several of the world's leaders rose up and blamed the aliens for the catastrophe. The popular opinion was that the aliens came to destroy our capability to defend ourselves against them in the inevitable invasion. The United Nations Security Council quickly passed resolutions behind closed doors authorizing deadly force to repel the aliens from our planet. They appointed a Colonel from Vladivostok, Russia, by the name of Vladimir Sikorsky, to lead the human armies against the aliens. His second in command was Huang Tan from China. Other nation states joined the effort and appointed military commanders and astronauts to oust the aliens called the Akarzdamedians and then to take the war to their doorstep.

"Colonel Sikorsky, his two sons and daughter showed humanity how to fight back. They attacked the Akarzdamedian space ship that had landed in Moscow, Russia. After a short battle Sikorsky and his forces took the craft from the aliens and executed the majority of the crew. Huang Tan and his forces did the same in Beijing, Hong Kong and upper Manchuria. Keira Brey led a Special Forces strike in Dublin and captured the alien ship that had landed there. Thomas and Theodore DeMartino led the forces in Seattle, Washington. The list of humans that rose to the challenge is exhausting. It was our proudest moment as we became one as a species to fight the common enemy.

"After all of the invading alien space crafts had been taken by force, Colonel Sikorsky ordered that the human forces fly those captured space craft to planet Akarzdamedia and conquer the entire species. Humanity was unanimous in their resolve to show the aliens that we would fight back and avenge the fallen. All of the space craft that humanity possessed was ordered to join the invasion, including the Calypso. So I ordered the course of the Calypso changed and we followed the armada of giant Akarzdamedian warships to a distant solar system.

"And the battle began.

"Colonel Sikorsky was ruthless. He ordered that humanity carpet bomb the major population locations of planet Akarzdamedia using nuclear missiles. Millions perished. My crew and I had very little in the way of offensive weaponry, so we orbited the planet and scanned the kill zones, charting the war between planets from a distance. As the deadly onslaught continued I was contacted by a leader of the Akarzdamedians. She identified herself as a Queen and stated that her name was

Danu. She begged for me to intervene and sue for peace between our people. She wanted to surrender to avoid further loss of life.

"So in an effort to end the bombing, I contacted Colonel Sikorsky and informed him that the slaughter should end and suggested that we enter into negotiations for a peace treaty. Instead of warmly receiving my request, Sikorsky cursed at me and refused to consider letting the Akarzdamedians off so easily. I asked the other commanders of the armada to consider opening a dialogue with the Akarzdamedians. Only Keira Brey from Ireland seemed receptive to the idea. The rest were so inflamed with desires of retribution over the destruction of the African Continent that they refused to consider mercy.

"I told Sikorsky that I would request clarification from the United Nations Secretary General regarding the extent of his mandate to make war on the aliens. That was the biggest error of my life. I had misjudged Vladimir Sikorsky as a commander and as a man. Sikorsky immediately declared me an enemy to the United Nations and he ordered the armada under his command to launch nuclear missiles at the Calypso. All save commanders DeMartino and Brey fired upon my ship and crew. Javier Perez Guerrero and I did our best to avoid the heat seeking nuclear weapons. My daughter, Judy, suggested we fly between the binary stars in an attempt to use the heat from the suns to draw off the missiles.

"We took her advice. We flew the Calypso at speeds that were faster than she had ever attained. I still recall how difficult it was for me to hold the steering column tight in my hands. The ship shook violently as we tried to avoid destruction. We were able to get within range of the largest star and her gravity began to pull on the Calypso. The stress of the speed and the gravitation tested my strength as nothing else ever had. And then, without warning, the stars disappeared.

"We were all at peace.

"I was a scientist and never believed in a God, but my first thoughts were that we were in heaven or some equivalent. Time was no longer a linear progression. My daughters and I became immortal in some way. Perhaps we slid into an alternate dimension or time line. Perhaps both, but it was peaceful and beautiful. The colors appeared first and then the angels came to us and told us we were safe. Words cannot describe the feeling of love that surrounded us all.

"And as the next two hundred years passed, Javier, my daughters, my other crew members and I watched humanity from a great distance. We watched as Vladimir Sikorsky became the conquering hero of planet Akarzdamedia. He was able to subjugate the alien survivors and steal their advanced technology for his own use. Sikorsky used his position as hero to the people to set himself up as the Secretary General of the United Nations. He soon became the leader of all humanity and ruthlessly consolidated his power. One by one, the other commanders of the Akarzdamedian Invasion perished.

"Sikorsky used stolen alien technology to expand his

influence to other solar systems. The Akarzdamedians had learned how to bend space and had converters to use the dunkle materie, dark matter, so that their space craft could reach speeds in space that we never believed possible. And that is when the rest of the existing species in the neighboring solar systems should have been afraid. They were all in grave danger from the expansion minded Sikorsky.

"He invaded solar system after solar system, planet after planet and enslaved the indigenous populations. Billions of life forms would be wiped out by the human military forces under the command of the Glorious Leader, Vladimir Sikorsky. The atrocities committed by the human race were numerous and the victims cried out for mercy. Their pleas went unanswered.

"My family and I watched the horror from our safe haven. I hoped and prayed that one day a hero would come of age to challenge Sikorsky and his reign of death. My daughters and I waited for almost two hundred years for that man or woman to come. To our mutual joy, the hero did come. But the hero was not just one man or woman. It would be many and they would be an unlikely band of military academy cadets that would become the catalyst for revolution. All of humanity would watch the bravery of these cadets as they fought for their very right to live on an abandoned lunar post called the Blood Moon. Human populations from settlements in eight solar systems would gain inspiration from the example of those cadets and they would rise up in the greatest civil war in the history of humanity.

"But to understand those heroes that battled on that Moon, it is necessary to understand where they came from and who they were. Part of that understanding begins aboard the United Nations Space Command Battle Cruiser Argonaut. Three very special young boys would establish a friendship that would one day challenge the draconian rule of Vladimir Sikorsky. The boys would create a loose association of friends that would be used by fate or the Gods to give hope to others when only despair existed before. Those cadets would give men and women the fire in their hearts to seek out true freedom and self-determination.

"I tell you now the story of those brave cadets. I begin their tale in the year of Sikorsky, 2516. My family and I await the day that we may be able to return to you with our historic vessel, the Calypso, and usher in a new age of peace and justice. For those of you that desire peace and freedom I ask you to hold on just a little longer. Your time is coming."

CHAPTER ONE

Although they had been superior in intellect, they had been no match for the parasitic life forms that practically wiped out their race. They had been known as the Danaraja, and over the centuries they had developed into a scientifically advanced society that explored dozens of solar systems. Their space craft had traveled to the farthest reaches of their galaxy. The Danaraja thirsted for knowledge as opposed to conquest. They desired to explore other worlds and learn from them.

Centuries ago, the once proud and powerful Danaraja had mastered space travel. They designed and constructed massive ships to break the speed of light and reach out across the universe. The Danaraja had built thousands of these large craft that were capable of long distance travel. They had landed on numerous planets and satellites, explored asteroid belts, suns, nebulas and other phenomena. They observed other stars in stages of early formation and recorded and collected data as other stars died.

The Danaraja also learned that the Universe was not a

safe place. Dangers lurked in locations that one would least expect. One of their craft had met with disaster after the crew encountered another species on another world in a solar system that was not their own. The new species was not one smarter than the Danaraja. It was one that had no concept of the value of life. It was a species that had only the basic of instincts, to survive, reproduce and feed. The hunger of this race knew no limits.

The Danaraja crew brought specimens of this new species aboard one of her massive space crafts after exploring a new planet. The species slowly took over, killed the Danaraja explorers and multiplied. The Danaraja crew, all seven hundred of them, became a part of the food chain and were devoured one by one.

The unfortunate large, grey, metallic ship from the Danaraja had drifted past the Wolf 359 Star System had been dead in space for about 100 years. None of the Danaraja crew was left alive. Only the alien species populated the ship. The carnivorous flesh eaters had multiplied and waited in the derelict ship for another life form to come. The decades passed since the creatures had last eaten. They waited in the dark areas of the large space craft to strike.

They spent the time in wait for another species to arrive so that they could feed again.

Humanity had never crossed paths with the alien race known as the Danaraja until one tragic day, in the year of

Sikorsky 2516.

New Edinburgh was an earth like planet that was early in its formation. It had been discovered and partially conquered by the Earth Space Command in the year of Sikorsky 2509. The planet was still deadly due to the indigenous population of predatory creatures, similar to the Jurassic and Triassic periods on ancient Earth. The men and women that sought to settle this new world had to travel far. But the journey through space was not the only risk potential settlers of this new world had to endure. Once the humans arrived to planet New Edinburgh they were faced with constant attacks from the flesh eating creatures that populated the land, air and sea. The early settlers had built barricades for protection from the dinosaur type creatures, the ever present aggressive flying carnivores and the many poisonous large insects that attacked without warning. The Space Command, in an effort to support and strengthen its' position on New Edinburgh, transported thousands of Marines, armed infantry, scientists, pilots, engineers, terra-form experts, weapons experts, medical personnel and even more civilian settlers. In addition, they increased the supply of weaponry for the soldiers on the ground to prosecute the war against the indigenous population.

The transports used were generally the United Nations Space Command Battle Cruisers. These were the finest ships of their time. Each Battle Cruiser was five decks high. The Battle Cruisers of Earth varied in size, but in general each of the space faring vessels were measured by a length of a fifteen thousand two hundred feet and the width of one thousand nine hundred feet. One of those large warships, the *Argonaut,* and her crew would be the first to make contact with the remains of the Danaraja species.

The *Argonaut* had been designed, constructed and maintained by engineers and technicians from the family owned and operated Fenster Corporation. The business was one of the most powerful and influential manufacturers of weapons and space craft in the history of mankind. In the days that followed the collapse of one of Earth's nations, the United States of America, all of the assets were auctioned off to other nation states and private investors or companies. The Fenster family purchased and took control of the old NASA facilities located in Texas. The family used the NASA drawings, plans, discoveries and computer systems to create an Armada of space ships, of different sizes and varying purposes, to sell to the highest bidders. The space craft were further advanced by stolen technology of alien races that humanity had fought and beaten during inter-solar system battles. Man had become the aggressor in the Universe, taking what it wanted from other worlds and enslaving the surviving inhabitants. The *Argonaut* was one of the proudest achievements of the Fenster Corporation due to the length of time she had been in service and her ability to wage war on other planets.

While in route to this new world, the computer on the

United Nations Space Command Battle Cruiser *Argonaut* detected an alien vessel floating in space.

The *Argonaut* computer alerted the Captain of the ship, who had been asleep in his quarters when the alert roused him from bed, that there was another ship in their vicinity of space. The Captain sat up in his bed when he heard the chime and verbal alert from his ship's automated communication system. His four wives and twenty-one children were safely in cryo-sleep in one of the lower levels of the Battle Cruiser. The computer created a three dimensional view of the Derelict ship in the center of the Captain's twenty by thirty foot quarters and a list of the schematics of the alien ship. The images before him were glowing in a light green color to act as an offset to the dark floors and grey walls of the room. The Captain carefully studied the three-dimensional diagram of the Derelict and listened to the verbal computer report of the distance, size, shape and make of the alien vessel. He paced his quarters, gazing out his transparent metal observation windows at the distant stars and darkness of deep space.

"For the computer historical archives, this is Captain Janos Janicek recording, commander of the United Nations Space Command Battleship Argonaut." Janicek had been trained well and with his vast experience he understood the concept of covering ones rear end. Each decision or command he issued had best be documented fully for protection of the staff if something went wrong. The current government would always find a scapegoat to punish in the event a mission resulted in disaster and Janicek was a master at ensuring that he was never that person.

"We have encountered a small alien derelict vessel in space. We are still four days travel from our destination to the Planet named New Edinburgh, also called the purple planet. Most of my crew is in cryo-sleep. I have a company of ninety-eight Marines awake and ready for service as well as twelve pilots, seven engineers, some medical doctors, nurses, scientists, fourteen computer technicians and the flight command personnel.

"The civilians for the most part are also in cryo-sleep. Some of the children are still awake, those that are the off-spring of the service men and women that remain on duty. There have been no incidents regarding the twelve Transport ships we are escorting to New Edinburgh. Last report is that all of the civilians on the transport ships are anxiously anticipating arriving at their new planet.

"Pursuant to General Order Number Seven Hundred Ninety-One as promulgated by the Glorious Leader, United Nations Secretary General Vladimir Sikorsky, I am ordering that we investigate this alien ship and board her if possible. If there are any alien life forms on board we will capture and detain pursuant to General Order Number Seven Hundred Ninety-Three. If there is any advanced technology on the space craft we shall seize it and ensure that it is safely delivered to Sikorsky's

Planet for investigation pursuant to General Order Number Seven Hundred Ninety-Four." Janicek ended his report and gazed out at the stars through the transparent metal observation windows in his quarters. He showered and ordered the computer to brew him a cup of coffee. He quickly dressed, cognizant that his command crew would be waiting for him on Level One, also referred to as the Command Station.

Janos Janicek was as proud of his ship and crew as a Captain could be. The *Argonaut* was one of the most decorated Battleship Cruisers of the entire Space Command. It had the ability to transport over two thousand eight hundred people. The lower cargo bays had three hundred one man fighter ships and twenty-seven Transport Ships called Raumschiff's. The *Argonaut* was fitted with all of the modern weaponry produced by the major family owned Corporations known as the Allen, Fenster, Breckenridge and the Rosenburg Corporations, to include long and short range nuclear missiles, long and short range rockets, laser batteries and bombs. She was certainly a force to be reckoned with in battle. The Battle Cruiser had the capability to carpet bomb a small planet or lunar body and then invade to obtain control over that astral body. She also had a compliment of engineering officers, computer technicians, tactical officers, science and medical personnel. Each of the U.N.S.C. Battle Cruisers was run from the Command Station on the Top Level, or Level One as it was referred to by the crew.

The only criticisms Janicek had of his ship were the

lousy food and the stale smell of the recycled air. Janicek kept his quarters full of nice smelling scents so he would avoid the foul stench of the regenerated oxygen. While on duty, he would endure the smell of the air on Level One as his scents would sometimes be too strong for other crew members to tolerate.

Janicek left his quarters, pulling on his deep blue colored turtle neck sweater. His Captain's insignia was a gold patch sewed into the left side of the collar of the turtle neck sweater. The left shoulder had a patch indicating the logo for the U.N.S.C. *Argonaut*. His white pants were cuffed at the ankle, covering a portion of his black service boots. The pants had a black utility belt with a hand laser attached and a small Fenster Corporation Holographic Communication device, called a Holo-com, which was used for long range dialogue. The Holo-com would allow individuals to see three dimensional views of the persons involved in the discussion. The temperature of the ship was regulated from the life support section located in the engine room. Each ship was kept at a constant sixty-five degrees, so the uniforms were warm and jackets for the military service men and women were optional while on board any ship for crew members that found the ship too cool for their comfort.

Janicek entered the hallway leading to one of the elevator lifts to Level One. The floors and the walls were all made from an impenetrable metal alloy that had been discovered on Sikorsky's Planet over a century ago. The floors had running carpets of different colors to add to the ambience. On the walls were pictures and paintings of past battles and decorated war heroes. Some portraits of the United Nations Secretary General and top ranking officials adorned the metallic walls. Their eyes seemed to follow a persons every movement.

Waiting for Janicek at the elevator lift was Doctor Jose Antonio de la Fuente Rios, the *Argonaut's* commanding medical officer. Rios was bald, standing about five feet seven inches tall. He was fifty-three years old. His uniform was almost identical to Janicek, except Rios' turtle neck sweater was white and he carried no laser pistol due to his oath as a physician to do no harm. His turtle neck had a rank of Army Colonel, which was a silver Eagle design. Rios had been married twelve times and had numerous children and grandchildren. Most of his family remained on Earth in the Argentina Territory where he had been born and raised. His two youngest wives, who were younger than Rios' oldest child, were on the ship and sleeping in the cryo-sleep chambers. Rios did not mind the General Orders of the Glorious Leader Vladimir Sikorsky, which required men of means to take on more than one spouse. The rule had been necessary due to the massive difference in the ratio of women to men. Over the last several decades, women had grown to outnumber men by over eight to one. Rios believed that the huge number of females was due to the medications given to stimulate more egg production for women and more sperm for men. The demand for an increase in births was due to the growing number of planets that humanity had conquered. Colonists were needed to settle those new worlds as well as soldiers to subjugate them. Rios had been educated at the Boston College of Medicine and had written on issues involving duplication or cloning of other mammals, to include humans. He had received many scientific awards for his theories and discoveries on the subject of copying life forms.

"The Computer Alert woke me up and indicated we have a ship of unknown origin close by. What kind of ship is it?" Rios inquired.

Janicek nodded, "I am going to Level One to get a look. Most of the Command staff is already there."

Rios followed the Captain into the elevator. Rios and Janicek had served together for several years and their friendship had grown strong over that extended time period. The individuals that served in the Space Command would grow closer than brothers and sisters given the weeks, months and even years they would spend trapped inside the metal shell of the space vessels they occupied. During their service, Rios and Janicek had seen spectacular new worlds and phenomena. Both men had long since passed the time for retirement, but loved the service and refused to depart their current lifestyle. Rios was aware that his friend would soon be promoted to Admiral and would be transferred to command an entire Fleet of Battle Cruisers. Rios believed that Janicek would make a fine Admiral and would be honored to serve under his leadership if asked to do so.

The trip to Level One was rapid. Due to their many years of service, both Dr. Rios and Captain Janicek were acclimated to the speed of the ascent of the elevators on the *Argonaut*. Most new crew members would become dizzy; some would even feel as if they were going to vomit at the end of the ride. Janicek had suggested to the Space Command that all Academies provide training to the cadets to prepare them for the speed of the elevator lifts. He was certain that the top brass ignored his suggestions as each year some new officer or crew member would complain about the speed and the resulting effect on them.

The elevator doors slid open to reveal the large, fifty yard long, forty yard wide, three balconies and ninety foot high ceiling of the Command Station. There were several crew members waiting for their Captain to arrive so that the mystery of the derelict space ship might be investigated and solved.

"Captain on the Bridge!" The female Marine Corps security guard bellowed when she saw Janicek. She was wearing a camouflaged sweater and pants with black boots. She had a rifle laser slung over her right shoulder and a web belt that had a hand laser, a holo-com and a large knife attached to it.

Everyone stood to attention for Janicek.

"At ease," Janicek instructed as he approached his station. Even after many years as a Captain, he felt uncomfortable when his subordinates would stand at attention for him. In his mind, they were all equals and he was no better than the lowest ranking soldier on the ship.

The Command Station or Level One had a rectangular shape and three levels. Two elevators, one from west and one from the east as well as ladders in the event of emergency power losses gave access to the highest level. A marine corp enlisted man or woman was always posted at the elevator entrances per the General Orders found in the Military Code. Along the east wall were stations for the officer of the day in security, weapons, life sciences, and computers. On the west wall were stations for astronomical navigation, flight control, a flight command officer, and communications. The seats for the Captain, executive Officer, and three officers as the Captain saw fit, were located to the south of the Command Station. The north of the Command Station had eight viewing screens that would give the crew many different angles around the outer hull. There was a set of ladders that led to the second and third levels which were balconies for additional technicians or scientists to work on the large computer systems that stretched from floor to ceiling.

The balconies were each in the shape of a horseshoe with the north viewing screens located at the open end of that "U" shape. The edges of the balconies were surrounded by five foot high metal rails at the end of the ten foot wide balconies. The rails were for safety of the service men and women. The two balconies, each extending for only ten feet from the wall to the safety rails, allowed for the staff to see, hear and interact with the staff below them.

Janicek was not an imposing person as he was five feet

six inches tall, which was much shorter than the average man of his era. He was physically fit for a man of fifty-one years of age and had thinning red hair. His left arm was mechanical as he had lost his real arm in combat eighteen years earlier in an explosion. He had a metal plate around his left skull and his jaw was also mechanical due to the same explosion that cost him his left arm. He was promoted to Captain of the *Argonaut* when the ship was constructed and commissioned for operations five years earlier. It was his life dream to command his own ship. He was selected to command the *Argonaut* even though he had worthy competition for the promotion. Janicek counted himself a fortunate man to be one of the few to serve and receive the honor to command a Battle Cruiser since only fifty such ships were operational at that time.

Janicek turned to face his officers on Level One. His Executive Officer, Commander James Phipps, was forty-one years old and a twenty year veteran of the United Nations Space Command. Phipps was a fit six foot four inches tall man from planet New South Africa. He had risen in rank from the Space Command branch, first as a fighter pilot and then later serving in the military intelligence section, also called the militzia by the civilians. Phipps had a large family as well, three wives and nine children, all of whom were in the cryo-sleep tubes for the journey to New Edinburgh. Since Phipps was in the military intelligence branch, his turtle neck sweater was dark purple to indicate his section. Phipps had served with Janicek on other ships when he had been a junior officer. When Janicek was selected as Captain, the Space Command allowed him to select his executive officer. He chose Phipps immediately. Janicek had every confidence in his second in command.

Colonel Kenneth Charles Knox, who was called "KC" by his closest friends, of the United Nations Marine Corps, was in his mid-forties, a muscular man, with a buzz haircut and several scars on his face due to years of combat. Knox had been one of the United Nations heroes that fought against the Martian colonists during the rebellion of 2510. It was rumored that Knox had killed about thirty rebels with his bare hands during the battle of Mars City. Knox had been born on a Space Station and was orphaned at a young age due to a terrorist bomb that caused his parents to be swept out into space. He was serving as the commander of the Marine ground forces that would land on planet New Edinburgh and temporary Chief of Security aboard the *Argonaut*. He was widowed and had several children of whom he said very little about. It was well known that Knox was set to marry three women on New Edinburgh when he arrived. He had five hundred fifty Marines on board the ship under his direct command. Four hundred fifty-two of the Marines under his charge were in cryo-sleep for the journey to New Edinburgh. He stood with his arms crossed over his massive, muscular chest and watched everyone with intense eyes. His sweater was mixed with the colors black, brown, green and grey to signify that he was in the Marines ground forces.

The two enlisted Marines, one each at the elevators, were wearing uniforms similar to Colonel Knox. Each guard had a laser rifle slung over his right shoulder. Both were Lance Corporals. One was named McCavin and the other Idoka.

At the Flight Control station was pilot Lieutenant Alfredrick Snead. He had been commissioned three years earlier after he had graduated from one of the military Space Command Academies located south-east of Tacoma, Washington Territory, Earth. Janicek considered Snead lazy as the young Lieutenant would never volunteer to do anything he did not have to do. His hair was almost never neatly cut or combed. Snead's wrinkled, deep blue sweater was loose over his lanky torso. Janicek had given Snead a substandard review in his last evaluation. One would expect improvement after receiving a bad write up which would affect future promotions, but Snead seemed to care little about such things and failed to improve. Janicek had been told by Space Command that Snead came from a family with connections and, therefore, could not be fired.

At the Astronomical Navigation control was Lieutenant Diana Douglas, an attractive young woman from what used to be known as the United States. Her long blonde hair was shoulder length and curled at the ends. She had blue eyes and a smile that caught attention. She had graduated from Earth Academy located near Houston, Texas Territory, with excellent grades and passed all of her flight trials in the top of her class. She was entering her fifth year of duty aboard the *Argonaut*. She was single and had no children that Janicek was aware of. She spent her spare time reading computer manuals on aerial tactics and military history. While most pilots would be out carousing, Douglas would spend her time expanding her knowledge in preparation for her ultimate dream which was to command a Battle Cruiser of her own. She was wearing her neatly pressed military issued deep blue sweater, black pants and freshly shined black boots. As was her norm, she was professional and a credit to the service.

The computer officer of the day was Lieutenant Junior Grade Michael Todd Parker Green. He was a new crew member that had been added just before the current mission to planet New Edinburgh had commenced. He was naive as to the potential dangers of serving on a Battle Cruiser but he was a genius at computers. Green had graduated number two in his class at the Biloxi Military Academy and his Intelligence Tests indicated that in addition to being a computer expert, he could probably run the entire ship all by himself. He had short dark hair, dark skin, light brown eyes and a slender build. He stood about five foot nine. Janicek had caught him constantly cracking his knuckles and fingers. Green had come from a large family; his father had seven wives and twenty-four children of which he was the oldest. Green was the first in his family to opt to serve in the Space Command. When Janicek had walked into Level One, Green was multi-tasking, performing the communications function for the day as well as the computer section. He sported a deep blue turtle neck sweater that had the gold patch of the ship logo on his right shoulder and his rank insignia on the collar.

The assigned weapons officer that day was Lieutenant Junior Grade Rafer Tierney. He had joined the ship at the same time as Green. They had gone to the same Academy and graduated together and seemed to have a good working relationship. Tierney was a lanky six foot six inches tall with short blond hair, brown eyes and spoke with a slight lisp. Tierney had earned a black belt in tae kwan doe and was an avid marathon runner. He was raised in Wales from a middle class family. Tierney was not as intelligent as Green, but a good young officer with potential, nonetheless. He sported a burgundy sweater, the designated color of the Weapons Section.

"Mister Green, have you been able to establish contact with the derelict?" Janicek more demanded than asked.

"No response from the vessel sir," Green responded.

"Any signs of life?" Janicek said, turning toward Dr. Rios.

"No life signs at all. The computer scans reveal that the majority of the sections have traces of breathable oxygen. There are some traces of ammonia, fluorine and chlorine in what appears to be the engine room and some other limited areas of the ship." Dr. Rios reported as he read a three dimensional screen that gave an outline of the scans received from the mystery ship.

"There seems to be no gravity or power on this ship,"

Green added, reading from his screen which was showing a three dimensional view of the scans of the interior and exterior of the derelict. "The aliens that had built and flew this vessel must have been very tall as the decks are all about twenty-five feet high. I am attempting to splice into the onboard computer and see if we can gain some clues as to where this ship originated."

Phipps paced around the Command Section and turned his attention to Green. "Any matches in computer regarding the origin of this ship or the species that constructed her?"

"None, sir. This is a race we have never encountered." Green answered, his voice was steady which surprised Phipps. Most young officers were more animated or in awe of a new alien race or mystery. Green was taking it all in stride.

"Thank you," Janicek looked over the skeleton crew around him and did not detect from any of them signs of stress or doubt. Janicek turned his attention to Phipps, "Regulations dictate that we must always investigate any foreign ship for technology and information. Given that we are on a skeleton crew, we cannot send over a full team."

"Agreed Captain. If we did, we would delay our arrival to New Edinburgh." Phipps motioned to Colonel Knox. "Perhaps we could send over a platoon of the Marines along with some engineers, medical and science officers. They could assess the alien ship for any dangerous organisms and whether it is worthwhile to investigate further. If it has evidence of useful technology we could tow her in with our connection cables."

"I have two platoons that are not in cryo-sleep," Knox acknowledged. He was always willing to lend a hand to the Space Command when asked to do so. "I can alert Lieutenant Gorski to get her platoon ready to assist."

"Has this Lieutenant Gorski seen any combat before?" Janicek inquired. "Is she qualified to lead a first contact mission?"

Knox smiled at Janicek and leaned over the security desk that he stood behind. "Captain, in addition to her training at the Academy and in the Marine Corps, Gorski attended and completed the Spetsnaz training in the Ural Mountains. As each of you know, that training is one of the most physically grueling to participate in. Only a few are selected to attend it and even fewer graduate. She is one of our best young officers. I have every confidence in her."

Phipps smiled, knowing full well that the training to become designated as Spetsnaz was the most challenging in the Space Command. One must be physically fit and tough, well rounded physically, emotionally and mentally sound, to succeed in that two month long course. About eighty percent of those selected to attend Spetsnaz training failed the course. Phipps recalled that to qualify to attend the Spetsnaz training they would have previously been awarded a black belt in one of the sanctioned martial arts and be a marksman in hand lasers. Phipps already liked this Lieutenant Gorski. "Spetsnaz? She must be a born killer. Is she available?"

Knox glared at Phipps, "At ease, Fly Boy. She is very married and a mother of two. And I understand that her husband also graduated the Spetsnaz training. If I were you, I would watch my step. She is very attractive and I am certain her husband could get jealous easily."

Phipps nodded slowly as he took in the warning. Although loneliness on a long voyage led to crew members taking risks to obtain companionship, making advances on the wife of a Spetsnaz graduate was not a risk Phipps was willing to take on.

"I would like to tag along on the flight," Dr. Rios stated excitedly. Contact with a new alien species was the main reason Rios loved space travel. He wanted to go on the mission badly for that reason and that he was bored by the daily rounds of the ship. Going to see an alien space craft would certainly be a way to liven up his day. "I can have Dr. Shaw join us."

"Mister Green, notify Lieutenant Commander Fischer from engineering that he is to report to Docking Bay Three," Janicek ordered. "Colonel Knox, please notify Lieutenant Gorski to assemble her platoon at the Docking Bay. Dr. Rios, you and Dr. Shaw are a part of the team. I want the launch in thirty minutes. We cannot be delayed too much longer on our trip to New Edinburgh. There is a war going on down on that planet and General Murdock needs the extra soldiers and supplies. Lieutenant Snead, fly us within twenty thousand kilometers of the Derelict and then bring us to a full stop. Inform the transport ships to pull within ten thousand kilometers of us and come to a full stop as well."

Rios began walking toward the east elevator shaft. He loved how Captain Janicek was always decisive in his orders.

The rest of the crew was cognizant of the war on New Edinburgh. The alien races there were numerous and they were proving to be fantastic adversaries. The *Argonaut* had many weapons and supplies to deliver as well as more troops to crush the aliens. Janicek was on a thin time margin and would not be able to justify a long delay.

The ship computer sent out both voice and text messages with the orders of Janicek and Knox to the crew members that had been selected to reconnoiter the derelict ship. Melita Gorski received her orders from Colonel Knox to report to the Docking Bay right away. She pulled her grey turtle neck sweater on over her thermal t-shirt, picked up her utility belt and tightened it around her waist. She was five foot nine inches tall and had good muscle tone due to her strict gymnasium and martial arts training regimen. Her dirty blonde hair was down to her buttocks and she had to pin it up whenever she went on duty. Her eyes were a light grey and sparkled in the artificial lighting of the ship. She habitually spent a minimum of an hour a day at the gymnasium, working out and continuing her training in martial arts and boxing. In one of her desk drawers under lock and hand-print identification key was her knife collection that numbered close to one hundred. She had knives from all across the Eastern

European Block of old Earth.

The quarters that she and her husband were assigned to live in were large due to their two children. They had a master bedroom, two smaller bedrooms for their children, closet space, rest room and showers. No kitchens were afforded on the Battle Cruisers as all personnel, whether civilian or military were expected to eat the cafeteria food. Only the Weapons Section had its' own cafeteria due to the longer hours that section would require out of the members if a conflict occurred. The metal floor was covered with a white carpet. The walls were light blue and had some of their wedding pictures hanging here and there with pictures of the children. Both had their Orders of Commission framed and hanging on the walls as well. Their Spetsnaz Awards also adorned the walls.

Melita Gorski smiled at her husband, Lieutenant Nikolai Gorski who was sitting on the floor of their quarters playing with their oldest son, Yuri. Nikolai was six feet three inches tall, muscular and ruggedly handsome. His dark hair was thick and would sometimes cover his deep blue eyes.

Melita and Nikolai met at the Space Command Academy in Moscow, Russia. Their romance was lightning fast and they were married within a year. Nikolai had been born and raised in Moscow and Melita had been born in Estonia. Both had a mutual dream of seeing the universe and settling on a new world. Nikolai was two years older than Melita and he delayed entering the service so that she could graduate and he could finish his

Master's Degree. They attended Spetsnaz training together after Melita's first year in the Academy. They both accepted commissions as Second Lieutenants in the U.N. Marines and were assigned to work as security officers on planet New Edinburgh. Both of them commanded their own platoon of Marines and had orders to report to General Rock Murdock, who was the commanding officer over the invasion forces at planet New Edinburgh. Their transport to the new planet was to be on the U.N.S.C. *Argonaut* and they were under the temporary command of Colonel Knox.

Little Yuri was born while they were still studying at the Academy. Piotr was only a few months old and had been born on the *Argonaut* just after they had left Earth. Child birth during space travel was a common event for humanity and safer than it had been in the past. With the advancements in medical research and technology, the past fears that existed regarding labor and delivery in the middle of deep space were forgotten.

Yuri was six years old and many years ahead in his educational development. He was always smiling and very friendly with the troops. He loved to go with his father and mother to learn self-defense and martial arts. Melita and Nickolai decided to expose their sons early to the life of military service. They stressed to Yuri the importance of safety with weapons and to always be prepared to defend himself. Yuri had inherited his father's dark hair and his mother's grey-blue eyes. The child loved both his parents and enjoyed hearing the tales of the past from them, especially their missions.

"You have to go to work Mommy?" Yuri asked her as she was gathering her gear.

Melita hugged her child, "Yes baby. Mommy has to go inspect a new space ship."

"Ooooooh," Yuri smiled. "Can I go?"

"No sweetie, but you can watch Mommy on the Computer Monitor here and on the one at the Day Care," Melita told him. "I will be back soon," She kissed him and then went to Piotr who was fast asleep. She gave him a soft kiss on the cheek.

She turned to her husband, "Keep the kids safe until I return?"

Nikolai embraced her and kissed her. "Of course, you be careful out there."

Melita smiled and picked up her Bowie knife and Laser rifle sitting on the table. She twirled the knife in her hand as if it were a toy. "You know I can take care of business honey. Ya lublo."

And with that she walked out the door.

Doctor William Shaw was in his quarters when he received the order to report to Docking Bay 3. He was in his late forties, white, with light brown shoulder-length hair. He had a goatee that was cut close to the chin. He had dark eyes and a gold earring in his left ear. His ship uniform was white to identify him as a member of the science crew. He was a pure academic, never spending time in the gymnasium. He would always spend his spare time studying or researching. He had achieved a Bachelor's Degree in Chemistry, Master's Degree in Mathematics, a PhD in physics and a medical degree. He was considered brilliant by his peers and a snob by most others. He was very condescending to those that could not follow his conversation and he had little patience for others.

Shaw had been divorced four times and was now on his fifth marriage. His newest wife was in the back bedroom with their new "litter" as many would call it. His wife was a Kotek, which was the name given to some of the survivors of gene splicing experimentation in Poland many decades ago. A group of Eastern European scientists, using state of the art technology, bred homeless humans and spliced animal DNA into the eggs and fetuses. Their mad plans were successful and several new "breeds" of human were created. One of those were the Kotek, which were part human, part cat. They were known to grow as tall as a normal human, but their bodies would have a coat of short fur covering them all over. They all also had long cat-like tails, cats' eyes, sharp teeth and some even had the sharp claws. Their legs and arms were capable of bending backwards to permit them to run and walk on all fours, a form of hyper-mobility of the joints. But they were also able to walk upright as well. Many humans found these hybrid humans attractive enough to engage in sexual relations with them. The shock to the scientific community came when it was learned that the Kotek hybrids could mate, conceive and give birth to offspring with full humans.

Shaw's Kotek wife was named Catherine. Her fur color was solid black and her cat's eyes were yellow. She stood about 5feet tall when walking upright. En route to New Edinburgh, Catherine gave birth to a litter of five new Kotek kitten/human hybrids. Shaw was their proud and doting biological father.

Shaw knew the majority of people held him in contempt for what they perceived as bestiality. In the past, Earth had laws against animal and human sex acts. But no laws were on the books to cover relations with human-animal hybrids. Mobs had picketed and marched on the United Nations demanding action and for new legislation to outlaw human and Kotek sexual relations. But the Glorious Leader, Vladimir Sikorsky, never supported criminalizing such acts and the protests went ignored. Shaw, naturally, cared little of the opinions of the less enlightened mob members. To Shaw, they were uneducated humans that had no capacity for comprehending relationships such as his and Catherine's. Shaw believed the majority of humanity to be a collection of worthless fools anyway. His relationship with Catherine was the best he had ever had. She was brilliant in her own right and the physical part of their relationship was always an adventure. He was proud of the scratch marks on his chest and back that she gave him each time they made love.

Shaw walked into the back bedroom to see Catherine lying sideways on the bed, with their five offspring breast feeding off her six breasts. Her long tail was wagging up and down.

"Cat, I have been called to report for duty. They found a derelict ship that we have to investigate, see if there might be any new technology we can learn from," Shaw told her as he gathered his pack of scanners.

Catherine meowed, "I will be here waiting for you. Be careful."

Shaw leaned over to kiss her and she licked the side of his face from chin to hairline. Shaw loved it when she did that. Her tongue was rough, just like a cat. He walked out of the quarters, picking up some of his life sign reading instruments as he left. Shaw was excited about the mission, thinking of the articles he could write about this new find and the fame and money that would come his way.

Lieutenant Melita Gorski had taken the several flights of stairs down to the lower level of the *Argonaut* where the Docking Bays were located. She enjoyed the exercise that running up and down the stairs provided. She exited the stairwell on Level Five and proceeded down the south hallway, heading south toward the metal bulk heads that separated the rest of the fifth level from the Docking Areas. The massive walls slid open for her as she approached due to the computerized sensors capturing the pressure of her footsteps on the metal walkway. She walked out onto the rail on the third walkway on Level Five, Docking Bay 3. She habitually tossed her Bowie knife in the air as she walked, allowing it to twist blade over hilt a few times before she caught it. Each Docking Bay had three metal walk planks, all facing at the large Raumschiff's in port. The third walk plank was for observation. The second and first were for the engineers and technicians to work on the ships engines that were docked. The floor level was where the crews would board the Raumschiff's for missions.

Gorski stood watching the activity going on below her. There were some weapons and engineer technicians running in and out of the rear loading area of a Raumschiff below that she assumed would be the ship selected to attempt to dock with the alien space craft. She was proud that she was selected to command the flight that would be the first to board the alien space craft. She could not wait to return and tell her husband and little Yuri of the adventure she was about to take part in. It was her dream that one day she would be selected to lead an assignment such as this. That dream had been the inspiration for Melita Gorski to join the Space Command in the first place.

Lieutenant Commander Myles Fischer was checking solar cell energy levels for the *Argonaut* when he received the order to report to the Docking Bay. Fischer was forty-seven years old, held a doctorate in mechanical engineering and a master's degree in nuclear engine design. He had never aspired to be a commander of his own ship, so he never applied for those assignments as they came available.   He was content to work on these amazing creations known as nuclear-solar hybrid engines. He was a stout man, a little less than six feet tall, jovial and loved by his fellow engine room technicians. His family was back on Earth. He had six ex-wives and fourteen children. Each of his marriages failed as he always desired the long jaunts into deep space. One by one, his wives left him.

Fischer motioned for two of his computer technicians and two engine room officers to join him on this historic mission. His team gathered up their tool kits, and a few hand held computers. They walked at a brisk pace to the Docking Bay to assist on this new discovery.

Each Docking Bay had enough space for 11 Raumschiff's to be in port. The Raumschiff was created to navigate to the surfaces of other worlds and to transport smaller crews to other locations. They were fast, maneuverable, reliable and packed enough armament to fight a small war. Created by the Fenster Corporation over one hundred years ago, the Raumschiff could carry over fifty crew members comfortably. The Raumschiff could dock with other similar ships and could magnetically attach to other craft. The Raumschiff had loading bays on either side and the rear, rocket launchers and laser canons on the top, bottom and front and back. The front of the ship also had rapid fire laser capability for short bursts against smaller targets. There were always twenty-five emergency cryo-sleep tubes on each ship, a medical section for treatment, and fifty bunk beds for the crew to sleep in. The Raumschiff had plenty of space for meetings and the pilot's cockpit had seats for a pilot and co-pilot. Some of the pilot sections had a third seat for a tactical officer to use during combat situations.

Melita Gorski moved down the metal stairs to the second stair balcony. She noticed that several of the technical crew were checking her out. She descended to the first floor where her Gunnery Sergeant, Dale Austin Millard, was waiting for her. Millard was a man mountain, seven feet tall, solid muscle, shaved head and a large scar from the left side of his chin to the top of his skull. Millard had been involved in over twenty-five combat missions and awarded several medals for his bravery. Millard was over fifty years old but looked like a young thirty. He was both feared and respected by the Marines under his supervision. He had many children, all daughters, and he knew the look of lust in a man's eyes when they were in the presence of an attractive woman. Millard observed that the men were giving his Lieutenant that look.

"You want me to take care of the mechanics, Lieutenant?" Millard asked her as he saluted her.

Gorski returned the salute. She tossed her Bowie knife in the air and caught it by the hilt. She pointed the blade at the engineers and doctors near the Raumschiff, "Take care of the men, Gunny, I can defend myself. Our responsibility today is to make sure our platoon and the civilians all return safe." She put on her Red Beret with her Spetsnaz insignia sewed into the front. The Military Code required that the beret was only to be worn by a Spetsnaz graduate when engaging in a mission. Gorski noted that Millard seemed surprised, as if he did not know that his Lieutenant had been through that elite training.

Millard's oldest daughter had become an officer in the Marines and had attempted the Spetsnaz training. The requirements were so grueling that Millard's daughter dropped out after one week. Millard had raised his daughter to be tough and self-sufficient so his respect for Gorski increased dramatically since she had been able to complete such demanding course. His other daughters that were old enough to move on had opted for easier careers. Some had become pilots, others went into the civilian sector and some were married with children.

"Assemble the platoon. Get them all suited up in enviro-suits in five minutes we board the Raumschiff. We launch in ten." Gorski sheathed her knife and began walking toward the storage units for the enviro-suits.

"Yes ma'am!" Millard turned to the forty-four marines near the stairs, "Marines! Suit up! Enviro suits in five minutes! We launch in ten minutes! Move it!"

The Marines moved rapidly. When Millard gave an order they followed without question. Millard had kept the platoon active every day with ten mile runs, weight lifting, target practice, weapons training and self-defense. The forty plus enlisted men and women moved to the lockers, retrieving grey enviro-suits, boots, oxygen tanks and gloves.

Sergeant Steven Hilts, Sergeant Thomas Silver, Lance

Corporal Lamarcus Spiller and Sergeant Rodger North, the four squad leaders, barked orders to their units. All four of the men had been born, raised and trained on old Earth. Most of them had joined the Marines for adventure, notoriety, good pay, medical benefits and to see other worlds. All four had some experience in combat situations. But the majority of the forty other platoon members had little to no experience in a hostile environment. The squad leaders knew that it was their duty and responsibility was to keep their men and women focused on the mission at hand.

The enviro-suits were created by the Breckenridge Corporation. The design was based on old earth technology but perfected so that a human could spend hours out in space and have more freedom of movement than space suits of the past. The Breckenridge enviro-suits were not bulky and had separate connections for the oxygen tanks, space safety gloves, space gravitational boots and weapons harnesses. The enviro-suits were easy to slip into and had light paper thin metal on the interior, a design that was necessary due to the constant dangers of deep space. The metal inside the enviro-suit was so light that it would move easily with the contours of the body. The helmet to the enviro-suit was made of a special transparent metal, allowing the man or woman in the suit a full view of their surroundings. The helmet securely connected inside the neck apparatus of the enviro-suit.

The forty Marines, squad leaders, Millard and Gorski

suited up quickly and retrieved laser rifles from the supply section. The laser rifles were four and a half feet long, able to fire bursts of deadly laser fire and had a function for a flame blast. There was also a connection that could be used to fasten a knife to the end of the barrel and use it as a bayonet. Gorski directed the platoon to take several thermite grenades, knives and laser pistols as well.

As the Marines were securing their weaponry, Dr. Shaw and Dr. Rios approached Gorski. Shaw was laughing as he watched the female platoon leader directing her Marines.

"Lieutenant, don't you think you are going a little overboard with all of the weapons you and your platoon are bringing?" Rios asked surveying all of the activity of the Marines.

Gorski faced Rios and Shaw, "With all due respect, Doctor, this mission is under my command until the derelict is secure and declared safe. I will take each and every precaution to ensure your safety and the safety of my platoon."

Shaw chuckled in a manner that demonstrated his contempt for female officers. "It's a dead ship. No life signs. No signs of any threat. You military types are hysterical."

Gorski stepped in front of Shaw and glared at him. She had met his type before while at the Academy and therefore knew how to handle the verbal abuse but he needed to understand with certainty and clarity that she would not allow his actions to place her platoon at risk. "Doctor, there may be no life signs that our computers can detect. But this is a vast universe and there are most likely billions upon billions of life signs we have never faced. Since there may be other forms of life that we have never made contact with, that would mean our computers would not detect them. Because of that fact, Doctor, this will be a military mission until the ship is cleared. That means I give the orders until further notice."

Rios motioned over to Lieutenant Commander Fischer and his technical team who were assembling some scanning devices and other tool kits. "Well, Fischer outranks you, so this is his mission. Not yours."

Gorski looked over at Fischer and his team of computer and engineer technicians, "Sorry to disappoint you Doctor. Regulations are clear that any original incursion on a newly discovered ship will be under the command of the Marines. When I find the ship is clear of any potential dangers then I will gladly turn the mission over to Lieutenant Commander Fischer. I will not turn it over to him until I am completely satisfied."

Shaw, still chuckling began to open his mouth to say something else, but Gorski cut him off. "Now, Doctors, get your enviro-suits on or this mission will leave without you."

Gorski turned and walked away from the two men. She found that Shaw was someone that she did not like.

Shaw whispered to Rios, "Who the hell does she think she is?"

Rios shrugged, "She's right, Bill. She is in charge. Do as

she says."

Rios walked away from Shaw to suit up. He felt badly that he had joined Shaw in challenging the Lieutenant. She carried herself well and seemed to be a no-nonsense officer. Rios decided that he should keep his mouth shut for now on and resolved to give Gorski a personal apology later.

Shaw clenched and unclenched his right fist. No woman had a right to speak to him in such a manner, he thought to himself. He was one of the greatest scientific minds of his generation. Perhaps of all times. Gorski was a mere woman and a grunt soldier at that. Shaw made a mental note to bring her up on charges for the insolence that she had displayed against him. He would make her pay for the manner in which she embarrassed him in front of Rios and the others.

The team boarded the Raumschiff *Jason A-1*. Most of the Marines took seats along the walls of the lower level on the ship, which were a long metal bench attached to the walls. Lieutenant Commander Fischer and Sergeant Hilts sat in the pilot and co-pilot seats respectively.

Hilts had been an officer candidate at the Academy when his low grades forced him to accept an enlistment. He had grown up in an orphanage as his mother had no husband and little money to support a child. The laws were clear in that whenever a parent could not afford to support a child the government moved in to place the child in an orphanage for adoption. He had no memories of his biological mother and he had never been adopted. Many prospective parents came and went to the Center for Abandoned Children in southern Montana. Each time the people came, Hilts was not selected and some other child or sibling group was taken away. He ran away several times due to the feelings of rejection he had experienced. When he had been apprehended by the authorities, he would be whipped or placed in solitary confinement due to his unauthorized runaway attempts. Sometimes he received both punishments. But he had managed to keep his school grades respectable enough to qualify for a slot at one of the military academies. While attending the college campus, he became enamored with the women and he spent more time chasing them than studying. Hilts had learned to pilot the Raumschiff's during his Academy studies before being academically suspended. Due to his flight experience he was Gorski and Millard's designated pilot for the platoon.

Fischer activated the thrusters and the computer, "Computer, perform systems check."

The computer answered within seconds, "All systems check out. Raumschiff Jason A-1 is clear for lift off."

Lieutenant Melita Gorski sat in the command seat that was located on the second level, one floor beneath the pilots section. "Command Station, this is Mission Commander Gorski. All mission crew are on board and accounted for. Requesting permission to proceed."

Captain Janicek and his Level One Command staff exchanged looks when they heard Gorski's voice. She sounded confident. Janicek nodded, "Permission granted Lieutenant."

Gorski gave the order to Hilts and Fischer, "Gentlemen, take us to the derelict."

The Raumschiff engines rumbled as the Marines and crew secured themselves into their seats with safety harnesses. Fischer and Hilts slowly guided the ship out of the Docking Bay and into the blackness of space. The crew could view *Argonaut* slowly growing smaller and the Derelict ship ahead slowly growing larger as the kilometers between them decreased.

Fischer looked at Hilts, "You are pretty skilled for a Sergeant."

Hilts smiled at the compliment. "Thank you, sir."

Gunnery Sergeant Millard had sat next to Gorski. After the *Jason A-1* left the Docking Bay, Millard looked over to his young Lieutenant, "I take it this is your first mission?"

Gorski nodded, "Does it show?"

Millard shook his head. He had served many officers in his career and she was the first that was a Spetsnaz graduate. It showed in the manner that she walked and spoke. She had a confidence about her that demanded respect. "Not at all Lieutenant. You are a natural. I especially loved how you handled those arrogant Doctors. In my entire career, there has always been a friction between the military branches and the science officers. What I mean is the doctors carry this arrogance with them, this air of superiority. They think that just because they went to college they are better than the rest of us. You cannot let them run over you. We were all watching when Rios and Shaw were trying to push you around. You stood up to them and that made the platoon proud of you. You are doing great."

"Thank you," Gorski swallowed as she could feel her adrenaline level rising as the alien ship grew closer on the three dimensional broadcast screens that were in every upper corner of the ship. It was her first mission and she hoped that she would be successful in bringing all of her platoon safely back to their mother ship. Her thoughts raced about the approaching alien derelict. Who had built her? What was her fate? How did she end up here, in the middle of nowhere? It was a miracle that *Argonaut* had even come this way and scanned this strange ship from another world. What advances in science would we recover? Would we learn of the race that had built her? Gorski focused on the mission. Her Academy Training taught her the three standing orders when boarding an abandoned alien craft. Secure the ship, ensure the safety of the boarding party, and recover all useable science and technology. All in that order. She was determined to do all she could so that her first mission would go by the book.

"You know, Gunny? Not all scientists are bad," Gorski said for the sake of conversation.

"Really, Lieutenant? All the ones I dealt with were full of themselves," Millard told her.

"My mother was a doctor of hydraulic engineering," Gorski said as she braced herself for the eventual docking of the

Jason A-1 to the alien craft. "She was one of the scientists that were involved in reinforcing the receding land mass near the Baltic Sea so that the land and water levels remained constant. She was brilliant and a great mother. I miss her very much."

"What happened to her?" Millard asked. He was surprised that his Lieutenant would open up to him in such a manner since most officers were very private about their personal lives. Her willingness to spend time speaking to him was refreshing, he thought to himself. Most officers would have nothing to do with the non-commissioned officers or enlisted ranks. She was different.

"A magnetizer crane malfunctioned causing a large slab of metal to fall loose at a construction site she was working at in Krakow. The metal weighed about two tons and it fell right on top of my mother and seven other co-workers. There wasn't even enough of her to bury. My father put a headstone up for her in our home town so that he would have a place to visit her."

"I am sorry," Millard said as there were more updates from Fischer coming in over the loud communication systems. "Did you have any siblings?"

"Three," Gorski smiled as she recalled the faces of her family. "They are all younger than me. When I left to join this mission I told them not to grow up to be arrogant scientists."

Millard laughed out loud.

"We are within fifty feet of the alien spacecraft," Hilts called out as he turned on the outer spot lights to illuminate the alien craft. He whistled at the size of the ship. He was in awe of the colors on the hull. There were geometric patterns of greens, yellows, reds and white all over the hull. The four colors must have had some form of significance to the aliens that once flew the space craft. Perhaps a flag color or some form of identification. "She's not as big as a Battle Cruiser but a good size nonetheless. Lieutenant Gorski, we are circling her for a good location to dock."

The Raumschiff went around the blind side of the alien ship with her spot lights revealing the damaged hull. Fischer speculated that the damages were from some form of meteor storm. Fischer leaned forward in his chair and pointed, "Sergeant, do you see that? It looks like a port."

Hilts looked at what Fischer was pointing at and nodded, "You're right sir. I believe we can dock there."

It was a twelve foot radius circle that was extended about five feet out from the hull of the ship. There looked to be a computer pad on the center of the circle that might be accessed by way of hacking into the alien computer. If successful, they could gain access through that location.

"Fischer to crew. I think we found a docking port. Hilts and I will negotiate attachment procedures. Since this is a foreign craft, it might be a bumpy ride. So, everyone sit down and strap yourselves in."

Gorski looked at Millard and pressed the command terminal button on the wall behind her to open communication throughout the *Jason A-1*. "This is Lieutenant Gorski. All crew, secure your safety harnesses and your enviro-suit helmets. We do not know what to expect, so take each and every precaution."

Using the half-moon shaped steering columns, Fischer and Hilts guided the *Jason A-1* to the side of the alien ship.

"Slowly," Fischer said softly. "Slowly."

It seemed like an hour passed as the two men took every painstaking second to negotiate the docking to the alien craft. Hilts was sweating due to the stress. One mistake could cause a hull breach on the Raumschiff and explosive decompression would end their trip quickly. Hilts breathed easier when the two ships finally came together. All of the mission team heard the sound of metal hitting metal, as if it were a bass drum beat.

Hilts was typing on his co-pilot console, "Activating magnetic docking clamps."

Fischer was also typing in commands on his console, "Full stop. Docking procedure a success. Lieutenant Gorski, it is now up to you."

"Marines, disconnect safety harnesses!" Gorski ordered as she unstrapped her belts and stood up. "Gunnery Sergeant Millard, assemble the squads to the docking port. Sergeant Hilts, I need for you to stay on board the Jason until further notice. Gunnery Sergeant Millard will lead your squad."

Hilts nodded, "Yes ma'am." He was disappointed that he would not get to lead his squad onto the new craft. But he understood that someone had to stay behind, just in case there was an emergency that required a quick exit.

Millard led the marines to the port doors. Fischer joined them and began giving instructions to the computer to extend the docking tube. The crew heard the sound of the tube extending and attaching to the hull of the alien vessel. Rios and Shaw stood in the background as Gorski approached, her laser rifle cradled in her hands. Shaw watched her pass him and he leaned over to Rios, "She really is going to treat this like a military operation."

Rios picked up his medical kit and hand computer. He was growing weary of Shaw's attitude of self-importance. "Cut her some slack. She's doing her job."

Gorski was motioning to Lance Corporal Spiller as she began to bark out more orders to her platoon. "When the hatch opens, your squad will enter first. Secure the area. You will be followed by Sergeant North's squad and then Sergeant Silver. We advance by alternating squads, each covering the other. Understand?"

"Yes, Lieutenant!" Spiller acknowledged. He knew his squad would be the first on the alien craft because his entire unit had been trained in computer hacking at a special training exercise. He was elated that his platoon leader understood the necessity of sending his squad in as the point and that she had taken the time to learn the talents and skills of the Marines under her command. Spiller felt his confidence in Gorski grow with each command she issued.

They all watched Fischer open the dock entrance of the

Jason and followed him down the hall way of the docking tube. Fischer was joined by Spiller as the two men began to splice into the alien door mechanism with their hand operated computers. Spiller had a hand held device that had several wires hanging from it. He attached the wires to the alien device and began speaking orders into his hand held computer. Fischer placed three one foot long square scanners on the round doorway and pulled out his hand held device and was scanning for life forms, hull breaches, gas and any other helpful clue as to what may lie beyond the round doorway.

"Detecting titanium, iron, lead, tin, zinc, nickel, molybdenum, gold, diamond, methane gas, oxygen, and some other gases," Fischer reported as he read from his small computer screen. "No life forms detected."

Suddenly, there was a sound of gas, like a hiss of a snake that moved into the *Jason*. The alien docking door slowly slid open, revealing a vast chamber.

It was pitch black inside.

Spiller and his nine squad members moved in, their laser rifle barrels pointing into the darkness. Their enviro-suit helmets had a light on the top, illuminating the dark interior of the craft. Spiller and his men placed magnetized lights on the walls as they moved in, their laser rifles at the ready. The chamber was quickly brightened by the magnetic lights. Sergeant North's squad came in next and Spiller's squad kept advancing. Soon, all of the mission crew, save Sergeant Hilts, was standing inside the alien craft.

Rios was inspecting the walls, "The metal is red-orange."

Fischer touched the wall with his enviro-suit covered left hand and the wall began to move and change shape. He cried out in fear and retracted his hand quickly. The wall disappeared to reveal a long, winding hallway. Several of the Marines stepped backwards, startled by the wall seemingly ceasing to exist.

"Be careful of what you touch," Millard said to Fischer.

"You don't say, Gunny?" Fischer smiled at him as he was a bit embarrassed at himself for reacting the way he did when the wall faded away.

Gorski motioned for Spiller to proceed. She turned her attention to two marines, "Irsay, Gibbs, you two stand guard here. If you observe anything out of the ordinary you alert us immediately."

Privates Irsay and Gibbs nodded that they understood as the rest of the team moved forward.

Spiller and his squad continued to place magnetic lights on the walls as they moved forward. Rios and Shaw were using their hand-held computers, scanning for life signs and the elemental makeup of the ship and for oxygen.

"Lieutenant Gorski," Shaw said loudly. "My instrument reads that this hallway is full of breathable oxygen. It is safe to remove our enviro-suits."

"Negative, Doctor," Gorski said quickly. "We all stay in

our enviro-suits until we secure the entire ship."

Shaw glared at Gorski as she denied his request. No one was supposed to speak to him in such a manner.

The members of the mission keep moving through the hallway. After a few minutes of walking, they encountered a large staircase going up and another set leading downward. It was about fifteen feet wide and white in color. There were red hand rails on either side of it. The stairs were straight up and down to the next levels. Gorski looked down at the pitch black below. She was not able to determine how far down the bottom of the ship was without lighting.

Fischer joined Gorski, Millard and Spiller at the foot of the stairs. They inspected the actual steps and found that they were longer than a staircase for humans. Generally, human stair steps would be a foot higher than the previous step. These were two and a half to three feet apart. Fischer speculated that the alien race that had built this ship were about double the height of a human.

"Preliminary scans indicated the engine room was down below," Fischer pointed out.

Gorski nodded as she received the information. "Very well, Lieutenant Commander Fischer, take your team downstairs along with Doctor Rios. Gunnery Sergeant Millard, Sergeant North, go with them. Dr. Shaw, you stay with me."

Shaw glared at her as he felt that only he had the right to determine where he went first. The female Marine was really testing his patience. "Where are we going?"

Gorski pointed the barrel of her laser rifle upwards. "While they descend, we will ascend. We need to determine what is on the upper level. And since you are not an engineer, at least none of the papers you have written indicate that you are, I thought you might be more interested in what might be topside."

Shaw suppressed the desire he had to laugh at the woman as he nodded. He doubted that she would be able to understand his papers on mathematics or physics. "Lead on."

Fischer and his group began moving down the large staircase. North had his squad members place magnetic lights on the stairs so that they could have a view of where they were going.

Gorski led her group upstairs. Spiller and his squad continued to place the magnetic lights around them to brighten up the stairwell. Gorski counted each of the fifty-five stairs they climbed before her team came to another huge chamber. They found several rows of large desks and chairs. Spiller and his squad placed several magnetic lights around as Gorski slowly moved through the room with her laser rifle at the ready.

Shaw swore as he tripped and fell to the metallic floor. He rolled over and saw a ten foot long skeleton lying next to him. Shaw screamed and urinated inside his enviro-suit.

Spiller and Silver helped Shaw to his feet. Gorski knelt down to inspect the skeleton. It was ten feet long and the bones were yellow-green. She counted four legs, four arms, and noticed that it had a wide body. The head was larger than a human skull, and seemed to have four holes for eyes. The teeth were dull.

Gorski looked over at Shaw, "Get a grip, Doctor. This is why you are here. We need you to assess the aliens' physical structure, their DNA, and see if you can determine a cause of death."

"Lieutenant, we found about twenty-five more skeletons," Spiller reported from the other side of the chamber. He lifted one of the large skeletons up with his right hand. "They are light. I can lift it with one hand without even trying."

Gorski pressed a red button on the right sleeve of her enviro-suit to activate her long distant communication controls. "Gorski to Argonaut. Do you copy?"

"We copy." Gorski recognized that it was Captain Janacek's voice responding to her. "Report Lieutenant."

"We have located no less that 26 alien skeletons on the upper level of the ship," Gorski said calmly. "Doctor Shaw will be inspecting them for DNA and possible causes of death. The upper level seems to be a command area; there are rows of large metallic desks and what would appear to be computer banks. We have found no offensive weapons at all. No uniforms either."

"Keep the broadcasts coming," Janicek ordered. "We need to know if the ship is biologically safe to take with us. Remember we have a deadline to get to the Purple Planet."

Gorski knew that the code word for planet New

Edinburgh was the Purple Planet due to her colorful purples that covered her surface. She did not like being rushed on a mission such as this one. Too many dangers could be around and cutting corners might be a deadly mistake.

Millard and North led the second group down the large stairs. They encountered several more alien skeletons on the stairs just like the one that Shaw had tripped over.

"What do you make of this?" Millard asked Rios and Fischer.

Rios scanned one of the yellow-green skeletons, "DNA is far different than ours. My computer indicates this skeleton is about 100 years old. I cannot tell the cause of death. How many are here?"

Fischer cleared his throat, "We count eighteen skeletons."

Millard was walking further down the stairs, "There are more here. I count another twelve skeletons. Same shape."

Fischer joined Millard and gave him a look mixed with wonder and confusion. "What the hell happened here?"

"A virus? A hull breach?" Millard speculated.

"We did not detect evidence of either of those probabilities," Rios said. "It could be a virus we never encountered. But..."

"But what?" Fischer asked.

Rios shined his lights up and then down, "Our readings indicated that the ship was airtight. Nothing could get in or out."

"So?" Fischer demanded.

"So, whatever caused this might still be here," Rios concluded.

Millard looked down upon the strange alien remains, "Let's move out. The faster we complete this mission, the faster we can get the hell off this ship." Millard hated mysteries. They gave him ulcers.

Gorski shined her flashlight up at the ceiling of the room and was admiring the artwork she observed. The aliens that must have painted the mural on the ship had a great eye for art. The mural was of a beautiful forest and a lake in the center. There were animals in the painting that Gorski had never seen before. She speculated the mural depicted the alien home world, possibly there to give the crew a reminder of home. Perhaps a way to help with the dilemma of being away from civilization for too long.

Spiller, Silver and their squads began scans of the computer banks, using devices similar to the one that Spiller used to open the docking lock. They located a total of sixty-seven skeletons on the upper level. Spiller activated his holographic keyboard from his small hand held computer so that he could type in commands with his gloved hands. The keyboard was about a foot above his hand held device and glowed a light blue color that reflected off the transparent face mask of Spiller. He had already attached his small cables from his computer to the alien machinery. He started typing furiously onto this holographic pad. Within five minutes there were colors appearing in the center of the chamber.

Shaw was still scanning the alien remains when Spiller yelled with glee.

"I think we are in!" Spiller announced with joy.

A holographic image of a crew of over one hundred aliens appeared before Gorski and her marines. They all had four legs, four arms, four eyes, two antennae and were about ten to eleven feet tall. Their skin color of the majority was green. Yellow for several others and two were red skinned. One of the aliens, a red skinned one, stepped forward and began speaking. It was in a language Gorski had never heard.

"Spiller, can your computers translate this?" Gorski said as she circled the holographic image of what she assumed were the alien crew of the ship. What were they saying? The ship was in the background. Was this an image of the alien home world? Were they talking about how proud they were to be chosen to serve on whatever their mission was?

Spiller was working on his small computer, typing furiously on his holographic computer keyboard. "Lieutenant, I cannot get my computer to translate. It has no frame of reference to this language. The cadence of the speech is foreign to us. There's no way until we have downloaded enough of their language downloaded before the computer can start translating the language.

"If only Champollion was here," Gorski mused.

Shaw shot a look at Gorski. He was surprised that a military grunt would know anything about Champollion or any other science for that matter.

Shaw moved over to Spiller and stood next to him. Shaw's jaw was wide open in awe of the visions before him. "We are recording all of this aren't we?"

"Recording and sending the transmission back to the Argonaut sir," Spiller assured Shaw as he was typing on his keyboard. "Maybe the Argonaut computer techs can get a good translation of what this guy is saying."

"I wish we could determine what he, or she, was saying," Gorski agreed. She smiled over at Shaw. "Congratulations Doctor. This event should give your lecture circuit career a huge boost."

Shaw gritted his teeth, detecting that Gorski did not respect his scientific research. He really disliked the female Lieutenant.

Millard, Rios, Fischer, North and their group made it to the last stair. They were in the center of a vast chamber. Millard and North ordered the Marines to start placing magnetic lights on the floor and walls. The chamber began to illuminate as the Marines followed their orders to inspect the room. One of Fischer's computer technicians indicated that they were in the engine room. They continued placing magnetic lights as they moved around the large engine control room. They saw rows of computers on each wall, chairs, desks and a high ceiling, about fifty feet up. The colors of the room were the same as the outside hull.

Fischer walked quickly to the computers, and was barking orders to his two female engineer technicians. They all began suing hand held computers, trying to hack into the alien computer just as Spiller and his squad had done upstairs.

Rios, walking into the center of the room, was holding his scanner up, and began walking in circles. The others could see the reflections of the elemental readings from his hand held device reflecting off his helmet.

"Detecting ammonia and methane gases here," Rios reported. "Strange, that neither of those two gases were detected on the rest of the ship."

"It might be because of some engine emission," Fischer speculated. "There are several other skeletons over in the corner."

Millard noticed that the marines were relaxing. Some of them were slinging their laser rifles over their shoulders and two were telling jokes. "Marines, stand ready. Look sharp."

The marines readied their weapons, although some of them did not understand Millard's hyper vigilance.

Rios continued his circular movements until he stopped and slowly looked up at the ceiling. He shined his light up and that was when he saw them. "Caesar's Ghost...."

On the ceiling of the engine room were millions of one to two inch radius life forms. They resembled colored golf balls.

They each glowed different colors when the artificial lights shined on them. There were many different shades of red, green, white, blue, yellow, orange, purple and mauve.

Rios motioned at the ceiling and was turning his head to the others that were with him. He looked in the direction of Millard.

"Do you see them?" Rios asked excitedly. "They are glowing, like fireflies back on Earth!"

Millard looked up at the ceiling; his eyes were wide with awe at the sight of the tiny aliens. "What the hell are they?"

Rios was scanning the strange glowing creatures with his small computer. "Computer has never encountered such a life form before. They are one to two inches around and about an inch thick. Their composition is completely foreign."

"I think we can start up the power!" Fischer announced proudly. He and his technicians were in the back of the large engine room and had been diligently working to find out whether the ship had sustained engine damage or some other tragedy leaving her marooned in space. They found no such evidence of such an event. They were all using human instruments and quickly deciphering how to initiate and operate the space craft.

Millard looked over at the skeletons of the aliens and then looked back at Fischer and his team. "I would advise against that, sir. In fact, we should probably slowly withdraw from here."

Rios looked over to Millard, scowling. "Withdraw? Are

you out of your mind? This is a new species! As a Doctor, I have an obligation to learn all I can of them."

Fischer and his technicians were true to their word, the engines fired up making a loud rumble followed by a humming sound. They cheered at their accomplishment.

In the upper level of the space craft, Gorski and her two squads heard the engine turn on. They could feel the metal floors beneath their feet shake as the ship came to life. "Gunnery Sergeant, what is going on down in the engine room?"

Lights were coming on all over the ship. Other computer panels began to light up with different colors. The Derelict shook as if coming out of a long slumber.

"Lieutenant Commander Fischer was able to turn on the engines," Millard's voice answered. "And we found a life form, millions of them."

Gorski looked at Spiller and Shaw and then down at the skeletons. "Damn. Millard, pull everyone out of there. Now!"

Shaw turned around and faced Gorski; his face was contorted with anger at her order to abort. "Are you actually going to leave this discovery? What is wrong with you?" The fact that Shaw despised the military was evident in the manner in which he snarled his words. Here, on this newly encountered alien craft, this was a chance for discovery and expanding knowledge which would be thwarted because they sent a paranoid military officer that wanted to run before any proof of danger exists.

"These skeletons have no clothing remnants. Look at that three dimensional recording that we found of them. All of this alien crew was clothed. I do not have to be a doctor to conclude that they all died of the same thing! What if that life form below is what killed this crew?" Gorski turned to Spiller and Silver, "Round up your squads. We are returning to the Jason. Move it."

Millard ran across the long engine room and put his hand on Fischer's shoulder. "Sir, you heard the Lieutenant. We need to make our way back to the Raumschiff."

Fischer shook his head no. "I outrank the Lieutenant and I am now taking over this mission. As of now, Lieutenant Gorski has no authority on this space craft. We are staying. This engine technology is far superior to Earths. We must take this ship in to the Purple Planet and study her. I think your platoon leader is wrong. If those new life forms were a danger, they would have acted already. Besides, they are so tiny. What can they do to us?"

As if the tiny life forms understood Fischer's question, a two inch round and two inch thick, light blue colored alien dropped from the engine room ceiling and landed on the face mask of Doctor Rios' enviro-suit. It stuck to his helmet, with little centipede like feelers touching his transparent mask. It had no eyes. It was just a blue, furry looking creature, almost like a colored cotton ball. It crawled around the face mask of the Doctor, moving around in a manner of no rhyme or reason.

"This is amazing, they are curious about us!" Rios was

laughing as he gazed at the small blue glowing creature just an inch from his face. "This shows a level of intelligence for the life form. Do you all see? Can you see it?"

Suddenly, the tiny alien secreted a blue liquid onto Doctor Rios' visor. The liquid slid over Rios' face mask like water on a car windshield. Within seconds, his helmet began to emit a yellow cloud of smoke. His face mask began to crack open and the small blue creature changed shape, becoming thin as a sheet of paper and slid into Rios' helmet, through the newly created cracks.

"Its' in my helmet!" Rios bellowed as the creature quickly attached to Rios' left cheek, dozens of little tentacles were feeling his skin.

"It tickles!" Rios was laughing. While his mouth was open, the tiny alien sprouted twelve long legs, thin as a daddy long legs spider and about three inches long. The legs moved lightning fast and propelled the alien over Rios' face. It swiftly slithered into the mouth of the medical doctor. Rios could not speak or scream because the alien slid down his throat and rapidly down into his stomach.

The rest of the landing crew watched Doctor Rios with awe, some with concern for his safety. Rios looked at Millard with a stunned look in his eyes. One of the female engineering technicians screamed in terror when Rios arched his back violently and reached for his stomach. He fell to the floor and began writhing in pain.

Rios screamed in agony as the tiny creature inside him began feasting on his stomach.

Several more of the tiny glowing aliens began dropping from the ceiling onto the humans below. The little aliens made a shrieking sound as they fell, similar to the annoying noise of a person scratching their finger nails on a chalk board. Everyone reacted by trying to cover their ears.

Millard urged everyone out of the engine room. "Run! Move out Marines!"

On the Command Station of the *Argonaut*, the skeleton crew could see the events from the broadcasts sent to them through the small computer recordings of Corporal Spiller and engineer Fischer. Captain Janicek turned to Lieutenant Commander Phipps and Colonel Knox and noted that both men had concern in their eyes. Janicek was biting his lower lip with concern and his face was pale as he was concerned for the crew that he had sent over to the alien ship. He was especially worried for his close friend, Doctor Rios, who was screaming in agony. Phipps was covering his mouth with his left hand, pacing. Knox was stone faced, showing no reaction.

"Tell them to withdraw," Janicek ordered. "Abandon the mission."

"Jason A-1, this is Argonaut. You are ordered to withdraw. Return to the Argonaut!" Green kept repeating the order, hoping his voice could be heard over the loud shrieks of the tiny aliens.

Janicek whispered to his executive officer, "Jim, raise Admiral Sikorsky from Space Command. We need to inform him of this incident."

After Melita Gorski had left the *Argonaut*, her husband, Nikolai had been ordered to have his platoon on alert. So, he took their children, Yuri and Piotr to the ship's day care facility before he reported for duty.

In the *Argonaut* Day Care, the nurse on duty had turned on the holographic broadcasts that were being transmitted from the *Jason A-1* mission. She did so since some of the children in the facility had parents that had bravely gone to make contact with the strange alien vessel. As the events unfolded, little Yuri Gorski watched with terror, knowing that his mother had boarded that ship. He pulled his knees up close to his chest and wrapped his arms around them. He glanced around the large day care facility. He saw a nurse in a white uniform changing a baby's diaper. There were two Italian boys, twins, that were about Yuri's age, kicking a soccer ball back and forth between them. The Italian boys were wearing a sports uniform that had the colors of the flag of their country. Other children were asleep, oblivious to the events occurring just twenty thousand kilometers away. Yuri wondered if any of the other children had parents fighting for their lives next to his mother on that mysterious alien ship. Yuri felt like this was all a horrible nightmare and he would soon wake up to see his mother smiling at him. Later in his life, Yuri Gorski would remember this moment as the first time he experienced true fear.

On the upper level of the derelict space craft, Gorski led Spiller, Silver, Shaw and the other Marines on the upper level down the stair case. Over their communication devices they heard the first scream of Doctor Rios as the tiny alien began feasting on his stomach and intestinal tract. As Rios was being eaten alive from the inside, he knew how the crew of the ship had died.

They were all eaten alive from the inside out.

Rios rolled around on the metallic floor of the alien craft's engine room.   He was screaming in pain as several more of the tiny creatures fell on him. The creatures spewed small drops of blue liquid on Rios' enviro-suit, dissolving the small areas just enough to allow the tiny creatures to slip in. Several of the flesh eating aliens slithered into Rios' nostrils, others down his throat as he screamed, others entered through his anal opening. One of the creatures began taking tiny bites out of his left eye.

Millard rallied his Marines as the tiny creatures fell down upon them like they were raindrops in a massive thunderstorm. Millard saw that Fischer, his two engineers and two computer technicians were completely covered by the tiny aliens. The aliens moved fast for their size. Their tiny legs seemed to grow in size as they ran along the walls, ceiling and floors, crossing great distances faster than a man running full speed.

Gorski yelled her orders over the cacophony of the alien noise and the screams of the dying.

"Hilts! Prepare for immediate separation and lift off! Irsay and Gibbs! Plant thermite charges in the hallway from the staircase to ten feet from the docking hatch! Put the charges on the floor, walls and ceiling! Set them to detonate manually!"

Hilts immediately began enabling the engine of the Raumschiff. He could see on his monitor what was occurring. His squad, his friends, were being annihilated. Irsay and Gibbs followed their orders, attaching magnetic thermite charges along the walls and the floor. Gibbs stood up on Irsay's shoulders to attach charges to the ceiling. Irsay walked down the hall, handing magnetic charges up to Gibbs so they could cover the ceiling in many areas. From the sounds of the screams, Gibbs and Irsay were concerned they would not have enough time to prepare an adequate defense.

As Millard led the remainder of his men out of the engine room the creatures followed. Millard and several of his Marines fired their laser rifles at the creatures. Millard heard Fischer's cries of agony as he was being eaten alive. Rios had been one of the Space Command's finest medical doctors, a brilliant man with vast experience and he was being reduced to the bottom of the food chain.

Fischer fell to the floor, swatting with futility at the hundreds of tiny starving flesh eaters attacking him. His death cry was high pitched as he writhed in agony on the floor. His technicians were suffering the same fate as the aliens were on them, their secretions eating through their enviro-suits to enable the creatures to attach to their flesh and begin their feast.

Millard realized that the laser fire would not be sufficient to repel the massive onslaught of the attack. There were thousands of them, perhaps millions.

"Marines! Switch to flame function! Burn them!"

Several of the marines complied and used their flame thrower function on their laser rifles. They were elated when several of the tiny carnivores burned under the heat of the flames. The screams the creatures made as they were roasted by the flames were even worse than their previous shrieks. Their long legs shriveled up as they were burned. Many more aliens dropped from the ceiling onto the survivors of the two squads. Millard felt several of them land on his back. Millard was well versed in the ability of the enviro-suit. He should not have felt the impact of such a small creature landing on him unless the small aliens weighed more than they seemed. He concluded that their density to size was deceiving.

Sergeant North was screaming at Millard for help. North was crawling on his hands and knees with about a thousand of the tiny creatures spitting their acidic blue liquid onto his enviro-suit. When the suit began to tear, the creatures slithered onto North, feasting on him with ravenous pleasure. Millard felt anger at North's death. He had first met North when the young man enlisted in the Corps. North was an excellent Marine in every way and he had been a good friend.

Millard kept firing his flame weapon with his left hand, and swatting at the creatures on his back with his right. "Lieutenant Gorski! I apologize for failing you! Use fire, flame weapons, thermite bombs and grenades! They can run on the ceiling and walls as fast as they can on the floor! Get off this ship! We are finished here!"

Millard felt his uniform tearing as the alien acidic liquid did its' deadly work. He could feel the creatures slithering onto his back. His other remaining men and women were screaming as they were being devoured. Millard removed two thermite grenades from his utility belt, flipped off their safety caps with his thumbs and pressed the detonators. He knew he only had eight seconds. He closed his eyes and knelt down on the floor. Thousands of the tiny creatures piled on top of him just before the two grenades detonated. Millard's death took about two thousand tiny creatures with him. The explosion caused the ship to vibrate. The two large balls of fire from the thermite grenades spread outward, in a fifteen foot radius.

Gorski, Silver and Spiller led their remaining platoon members and Doctor Shaw down the stair case. Gorski had to grab Shaw's arm several times, urging him to keep up. Gorski thought Shaw had a death wish as slow as he was moving. When Spiller and Silver were one flight of stairs from the hall leading to the docking area, they saw thousands of the tiny creatures moving rapidly up the staircase toward them.

"LT!" Silver yelled. "They are climbing up the stair case at us!"

"Marines! Use thermite grenades!" Gorski ordered as she pulled out two thermite grenades of her own from her web belt, one in each hand. Spiller, Silver and the other fifteen marines drew thermite grenades and threw them down the stairs.

"Fire in the hole!" Spiller yelled.

The thermite grenades burst in huge fifteen foot high and wide fireballs, incinerating anything within it's' circumference. Gorski noticed that the aliens on the steps were burned to a crisp. The creatures clearly understood that the Marines had the ability to fight back as they had momentarily ceased their advance. Seeing the lack of decisiveness in the attacking creatures Gorski ordered her men to unleash another thermite grenade attack. The soldiers complied with her order, each dropping another thermite grenade down upon the deadly aliens. The explosions caused more losses on the aliens and they retreated back into the engine room.

Shaw was frozen with fear. He could not move his feet, his mouth was dry and his hands were sweating. In all of Shaw's travels he had never been exposed to immediate danger such as this.

"Move it!" Gorski yelled and shoved Shaw forward. The two squads moved their feet, running down the final flight of stairs to the hallway. As the Marines all landed onto the hallway the hunger of the creatures overcame their fear of the fire weapons. They began to charge up the stairs, making their horrible screaming sounds again. Their hunger was insatiable since they had not eaten in almost one hundred Earth years. These final humans would not escape them.

Gorski and her platoon ran as fast as their legs could carry them. She saw that Irsay and Gibbs had followed their orders and planted many of the thermite devices. The two privates were waiting for them near the dock entrance as was Sergeant Hilts.

"Doctor, get on board the Jason!" Gorski pushed Shaw forward. "Hilts, are we ready for separation?"

Hilts nodded, "Yes ma'am. Are those things following you?"

Gorski turned toward the sounds of the starving aliens rushing toward them. "Roger that, Hilts! Irsay, Gibbs, get ready to detonate the charges on my command. Spiller, flank your squad on the right! Silver; flank your squad on the left. We need to burn them all. None of them can get through, or we are finished. Each of you understand me?"

They demonstrated that they understood by taking their positions. Several Marines dropped to a prone position, spreading their legs and leaning on their elbows, aiming their laser rifles in the direction of the approaching aliens. Other Marines knelt down behind those Marines and the rest stood behind the ones kneeling. It was a three level view of firepower. Ground, middle and ceiling. All of the Marines aimed their laser rifles down the hallway.

Gorski was proud of them. She knew they may not survive, but the aliens would be regretting the day they attacked her platoon. She had her laser rifle in her hands, prepared to join her men in the fight to survive.

On the *Argonaut*, Captain Janicek was alerted that a communication was coming in from the Fleet Admiral Sikorsky. Janicek pointed to the screens and Green put the broadcast for all to see. Janicek explained to Admiral Sikorsky the predicament.

Sikorsky was over one hundred sixty years old but he looked like a man of thirty years. He watched the displays he received from Green and showed little emotion. His orders were a shock to everyone in the Command Station.

Sikorsky shifted uncomfortably in his seat, "Captain, you know the Regulations dictate that whenever an unknown aggressive alien attack occurs, we must destroy them all. Those creatures cannot be allowed to reach the Argonaut or any Earth settlement."

Janicek faced the screen, "Admiral, it would seem that the commander of the mission might be able to repel the attack. We should at least wait and give them the chance to fight back."

Sikorsky shook his head, "Negative Captain. We cannot allow any biological infection to harm the majority. We do not know anything about these marauding aliens other than they are deadly to our life form. You are ordered to launch missiles and destroy the derelict ship."

"I protest! The soldiers over there are fighting valiantly..." Janicek began before he was cut off by the Admiral.

"You have been given a direct order, Captain! Destroy the alien ship and continue on your mission to planet New Edinburgh. No further delays will be tolerated! Sikorsky, signing off." His face disappeared from the screen.

Janicek turned and faced his officers, his lips were pursed. Janicek knew if he disobeyed the order, he would be prosecuted in a court martial by a military tribunal. His career would be over. Plus, he ran the risk of Sikorsky being correct about inviting a deadly organism onto the *Argonaut*. More lives would be at risk.   "Mister Tierney, you heard the Admiral. Notify weapons section to load two R5 Missiles and lock onto the alien space craft. Tell them to fire when ready." Janicek walked toward the elevator of the Command Section, his head down. His friends Rios and Fischer were dead. He had just issued an order to blow up about twenty-one brave souls. Janicek had faced these situations in the past. Command was stressful and also very lonely. It was not the first time he had been forced to issue orders that would end in the deaths of men and women under his command. He knew his orders today would haunt him for the rest of his life. "Jim, you are in command. I will be in my quarters."

Tierney complied with the orders. The R5 missiles packed more than enough explosive power to wipe out the alien ship. The R5's were armor piercing and would detonate from the inside of the craft. The explosion would be powerful and there would be no way the ship could survive. "Captain, launch should occur in two minutes," Tierney reported softly.

Phipps nodded slowly.   Everyone on Level One was silent. The sadness of what was about to occur weighed on all of them.

Knox excused himself since it was his duty to inform his Lieutenant, Nikolai Gorski that his wife had died in the line of duty. Some of the other Marines had family on board and he would give them the news personally.

On the alien ship, the creatures were scurrying up the hallway toward their feast. The humans had an excellent flavor and they lusted for more of their flesh. They were running along the ceiling, on the walls and the floor.

But, the humans were not fleeing. They were facing them, waiting.

Gorski was standing in the center of the hallway, flanked by Spiller and Silver's squads. "Steady, wait, wait." She watched the creatures move at them faster than their tiny bodies should be able to move. "Ready... Now!"

Irsay and Gibbs detonated the thermite devices. The explosions shook the ship. Two of the marines lost their footing from the concussion of the blasts but recovered to their feet quickly. Fire engulfed the hallway. The aliens screamed as they were burned under six hundred degree fire. Thousands died.

But, the rest of the alien horde kept approaching. Gorski

aimed her laser rifle at the mob of tiny aliens. "On my command, burn them all!"

Gorski waited as the creatures charged them. She felt responsible for the loss of her two squads below. Millard, with all of his medals and certificates, all of his experience and training he could not survive the attack of these creatures. At least Millard had been able to let Gorski know how to defeat them.

The tiny aliens were now in range of the flame bursts of the laser rifles. Thirty feet.

Twenty-five feet.

"Ready!" Gorski barked.

Twenty feet.

"Aim!"

Fifteen feet.

"Fire at will!"

The marines were more than happy to oblige her. Some of them shot flames onto the aliens on the ceiling. The others roasted the aliens on the walls and on the floor.

"Keep firing!" Gorski encouraged them. "Don't let up!"

It seemed to go on forever. But, in a few minutes it was clear that the tiny creatures were retreating, at least, what was left of them. Gorski was certain that she and her Marines burned thousands of them to death.

"We did it!" Hilts hugged Spiller.

The other members of the two squads were cheering at

their victory. But their celebration was short lived.

Spiller reacted to a beeping on his hand held Holo-com device. He pulled out his computer and looked at the screen which was flashing a warning. There were missiles heading in the direction of the derelict space craft. "Lieutenant, I am detecting incoming missiles." His face was contorted with confusion. "Who would have fired upon us?"

Gorski immediately realized exactly what had happened; her smile quickly vanished as she pulled her Holo-com device off her utility belt. "Gorski to Argonaut. Come in. The alien attack has been repelled. Repeat. The aliens have withdrawn."

Silence.

Shaw tore off his enviro-suit helmet, "Why aren't they responding? What the hell is going on here!"

Gorski looked over the men and women under her command. She deduced quickly that the Captain of the *Argonaut* could not take the risk of allowing these deadly aliens to survive. "I am sorry. The *Argonaut* command staff must have determined that the aliens were an unacceptable contamination risk. Those incoming missiles are meant to destroy this ship."

"And us?" Sergeant Silver was also confused. "But, we are winning. Don't they know that we are winning?"

"I am sorry," Gorski repeated with a touch of sadness in her voice. Her platoon had fought bravely and with distinction. "We all knew the risks of military service when we signed up. It was an honor to serve with each of you."

Spiller and Silver stared at Gorski with a blank expression, as if they could not believe that their own people would issue a command that would result in their deaths.

Gibbs and Irsay stood at attention and saluted their Lieutenant. Melita Gorski returned their salute, recognizing the respect the two Marines were showing to her with the gesture.

Shaw pulled out his communication device and began screaming into it. "This is Doctor Shaw! We are not contaminated! The aliens are defeated! Recall the missiles! Is anyone listening over there! Damn it! Answer me! Argonaut! Captain Janicek! Recall the missiles!"

What Shaw did not know was that everyone on the Command Station of the *Argonaut* heard every word.

Lieutenant Diana Douglas looked over to Lieutenant Commander Phipps, tears were in her eyes. "Can't we stop this? There is no reason for killing them. Please sir. Please."

Phipps shook his head, "I am sorry. There is absolutely nothing that I can do. The order came from an Admiral and cannot be rescinded."

"But sir," Tierney pleaded. "Admiral Sikorsky did not know that the team could defeat the alien attack. Call the Admiral back. Get him to reverse the order."

"I can't. It's too late," Phipps said softly just a few seconds before the two R5 missiles hit the alien ship.

Both missiles entered the metallic hull and detonated. The screen view showed a spectacular explosion of red, orange and white as the derelict ship was destroyed.

Phipps ordered the screen turned off and for the *Argonaut* to resume its' mission to New Edinburgh. As the large Earth Battle Cruiser turned away, they received a late transmission. It was from Lieutenant Melita Gorski. It had been a Holo-com recording the she had made just before the missiles impacted the alien space ship.

"Captain, I wanted you to know I understand why you did what you had to do. I would have given the same order in your shoes. To my husband, Nikolai, and my two sons, Ma armastan sind kogu sudamest (I love you with all my heart)."

Little Yuri Gorski sat in a fetal position watching the screens in the Day Care Center. He flinched as the alien ship that housed his mother erupted in an explosion. He watched as the screen went blank pursuant to Phipps' orders. The six year old child wept. He did not fully understand what had happened or why. But he did comprehend that his mother would not be coming back to him.

His sobbing attracted the attention of the Italian twin boys. They put down their soccer ball and each sat on opposite sides of the distraught Gorski boy. They put their arms around him, trying in vain to soothe him. One of the Italian boys said something in Italian to little Yuri, but he could not understand the words. However, it was clear the two strangers were trying to comfort Yuri in his moment of anguish. Yuri Gorski buried his face on the shoulder of one of the kind hearted Italian boys and cried.

Years later, Yuri Gorski would remember several lessons that he learned from his mother's untimely demise. First, the universe is a very dangerous place. Second, family is the most important thing in life. Third, trusting authority figures with your life was foolish. Fourth, one can find kindness in strangers. And fifth, those that fight by your side in battle are the only ones you can count on at that precise moment.

Those lessons would serve Yuri Gorski well into his adult life. They would define him in his actions as a man, as a student, as an officer and later as a leader. As the boy wept the two boys comforted him as best they could. The meeting between them would grow into a bond of friendship that would one day shake the Sikorsky family. Their names would go down in the annals of history as three of the greatest heroes ever. Yuri Gorski asked the two boys their names, but they did not comprehend the question. One boy seemed to sense that the distraught child needed to know their identities. He introduced himself as Marco and his brother as Dominic. Yuri told them his first name just seconds before his father appeared in the nursery.

The boy looked at his father and focused in on his face. It would be the only time in his childhood that Yuri Gorski would see his father shed tears. His father walked to him, lifted him in his arms and held him close. Father and son wept openly as the children in the day care watched them.

CHAPTER TWO

The space shuttle flights from planet New Edinburgh to Space Station Cy-7 were deemed safe for civilians and cadets. The last serious incident on a space shuttle occurred eight years earlier when a shuttle pilot, under the influence of an illegal drug commonly known as Red Dust, crashed into the New Edinburgh moon. All aboard died in the disaster. The Earth Empire civilian Secretary General of New Edinburgh, Alexander Lyss, began requiring mandatory drug testing of all shuttle pilots. The shuttles ran eight times daily and could comfortably transport up to two hundred fifty people, their luggage and packages.

Other than the drug issue and occasional engine repair needs, the flight control officers were always mindful of the infamous sandstorms that would occasional erupt. These were not the mild sand swirls that could be observed on Earth. Nor were they as violent as the dust storms on Mars. But, the sandstorms of the planet New Edinburgh had an electro-magnetic composition which would cause the space ship's on board instruments to give false readings. Pilots were known to crash into mountains even crashing on the ground, believing that they were still several kilometers from the landing strip. No ship was cleared for take-off if the climatology scans were recording evidence of a potential sandstorm.

The Cy Space Stations were named after the engineer that designed them, Cy Tyler Clemmons Johnson. They orbited most of the planets of the Earth Empire. The one orbiting New Edinburgh was the seventh one constructed. The Space Stations were built in collaboration with the estate of Cy Johnson, the Rosenburg Corporation, the Fenster Corporation and the Brackenridge Corporation. The stations would house over four thousand five hundred employees, tourists and temporary guests with ease. It was a large wheel design with spokes connecting the wheel to a center command area. The large wheel had approximately twenty stories, docking bays and one major station for space ship repairs.

Each of the space stations had the ability to extend or lower connecting tubes to larger space craft, such as the massive Battle Cruiser's or Science Exploration Type vessels that would attach to the space craft. Crew members of the connected space ship could walk with ease through the connecting tube onto the space station.

Space Station Cy-7 consisted of several hotels, bars,

restaurants, docking bays for small ships, transports and Raumschiff's. There were spacious living quarters for the employees of the space station, which included engineers, computer technicians, life sciences personnel, medical, Space Command officers, security guards, tourist guides, hotel and restaurant employees, mall sales clerks, shipping employees and members of the oldest profession in the Earth Empire, prostitutes. Cy-7 was a popular destination for military service members on leave from New Edinburgh as well as cadets and civilian employees.

The planet New Edinburgh was nicknamed "The Purple Planet" due to the sand covering the land masses being either light purple or deep purple. The humans from Earth discovered this new world and immediately set upon her, to exploit her natural resources and land masses. The indigenous population proved to be deadly to humans, but mankind had technology and was able to overwhelm the creatures of the new planet in the northern continent. Humanity had spent three decades populating eleven regions of the northern continent to house settlers from Earth. One of the eleven regions of the northern continent was named Clovis City. Most of the commerce of New Edinburgh was conducted there while the other regions were mainly used for farming and military defense. Clovis City housed the United Nations Administrative Building, major hospitals, military bases and the large Academy training young men and women for service in the United Nations Space Command. The large city was covered with restaurants, bars, businesses, large high rise buildings some of which were over one hundred floors high. There was a large landing strip in the center of the city which could accommodate several hundred Raumschiff space ships and transports comfortably. Other smaller landing areas existed throughout the city to accommodate any overflow in tourists or other travelers.

The entire ground of Clovis City was paved with transparent concrete so that the vegetation below could grow and the population could be safe from the deadly earth worms that enjoyed feasting on human flesh. The worms had been known to rise up from under the New Edinburgh soil, wrap around a human victim and then pull them under the ground so that the worm could crush and devour them. The early engineers and technicians had built in a few small rivers into the city which were stocked with fish for humans to catch and feed their families with.

There were many orange color conveyer belts which were about fifteen feet wide and would run from the United Nations Building to many other locations. One conveyer connected the United Nations Building to the main hospital, another went to the southernmost point of the Great Wall and another connected the United Nations Building to the landing strip. Once a human stepped onto the conveyer belt, they would travel at forty miles per hour to their destination. All over the city were statues of the Glorious Leader, Vladimir Sikorsky, that were larger than life size and the color gold. There were other statues for Sikorsky's children who were the top ranking military officers in the Earth Empire military command structure. Similar statues were scattered about for the heroes of the Racial Wars, but they were all stone and had no color. The Glorious Leader had decreed that his statues must always be more brilliant and eye catching than any other monument. At the large base of each statue of the Glorious Leader was the slogan "Weakness is Provocative" printed in bright bold letters.

The Academy on New Edinburgh had been named Clovis Academy, after the first King of France on Earth. It was a relatively new academy which housed about fourteen thousand eight hundred cadets from the ages of seventeen through twenty-four. To be accepted as a student in any military academy, such as Clovis Academy, the potential student must agree to a five year minimum commitment to serve in the United Nations Space Command. With that sworn agreement, a student could receive a four year Bachelor's Degree with the option of delaying commission into the Space Command service to study and earn a Doctorate Degree. The studies and training was intense, focused and demanding. Many cadets failed the training within their first year and were forced by their contractual agreement to enlist in the Marines or the Army. The cadets that were successful received a commission as an officer in whichever branch of the Space Command the graduate selected. Those graduates were drafted by the commanders of the Battle Cruiser Fleets to fill vacancies. After the Battle Cruisers made their selections the Science Exploration Vessels selected next, then the Naval Exploration UnterSee Boots, then the space stations, then the planetary ground forces, then the lunar colonies and then the worst assignments of all, asteroid stations.

Due to the stress of the training and studies, many cadets would carouse on the weekends at local bars on New Edinburgh. Or, assuming they could afford the rents and prices, spend a weekend on the Space Station Cy-7.

Some of the most frequent cadet visitors to the station were affectionately known as "Gorski's Gang." Their ringleader was a twenty-one year old cadet named Yuri Feklisov Gorski. He was in his last year at the Clovis Academy, a graduating senior. His gang was infamous for carousing, womanizing, breaking curfew, quick to jump into a fist fight, insubordinate and feared by the civilian population. The saying on New Edinburgh was that if Gorski's Gang is in town, hide your daughters. Several bars had been demolished over the last few years due to the brawls that would occur between the gang and their various opponents.

Normally, such alleged habitual rule breakers and nihilists would have been expelled from the academy and impressed into the enlisted ranks. However, each member of Gorski's Gang had maintained high grade point averages, were considered by their professors as extremely talented and showed exceptional leadership abilities in their own right. Plus, each member of gang were from prominent families. Yuri Gorski was the oldest son of Marine Corps Colonel Nikolai Gorski, the highest ranking Marine officer on New Edinburgh and one of the highest ranking Spetsnaz officers in the Earth Empire. Colonel Gorski was also a war hero, fighting in the Dinosaur Wars and keeping the peace since then on New Edinburgh.

Cadet Michel Darcel Evart was from a prominent, wealthy family in Saint Avold, France and his uncle was Major Sigebert Evart. Major Evart was also a hero of the Dinosaur War and was Colonel Gorski's second in command of military forces on New Edinburgh.

Cadets Dominic and Marco Andolini, twin brothers from Florence, Italy, were stars on the Clovis City soccer team named "The Rattlesnakes." Dominic Andolini had the highest scoring average of the New Edinburgh Futbol League. The Rattlesnakes were in the lead of their five team division and would play in the League Championship if they maintained their position. The Andolini brothers' father was a retired engineer and space ship repair technician and currently a consultant for a local engineering business. Their mother was a prominent politician in the United Nations on Earth.

Cadet Lester "Les" Brey Gillis had parents in the diplomatic corps on old Earth. His uncle was a Military History Professor on the renowned Academy located on the planet called Sikorsky's Planet. Gillis was also a descendant of some of the heroes of the Inter-Planetary Racial Wars against the aliens called the Akarzdamedians. He also happened to be one of the most intelligent students at the Academy, earning straight "A"s on all of his classes.

Cadet Drew Harrison was the son of an Admiral of the United Nations Space Command and one of the most physically powerful cadets. His mother had also served with distinction and all of his family had been in the military service at some point in their lives.

Cadet Drayton Love-Easter was the son of a major religious leader on Earth that had a massive broadcast audience, every Sunday, on every planet in the Earth Empire. It was estimated that Pastor Love-Easter has approximately two billion followers.

Those were the members of Gorski's Gang that were graduating seniors. Gorski and his friends had recruited several underclassmen and women to join their ranks. There were numerous students, but the major gang members were Jack Harcourt, Jen Staszko, Dirk Fenster, Archibald Frazier, April Mejia, Harumi Shigeta, Elektra Papanikolaou, Klaus Rhinehard, Rolf Rhinehard, Flora Darcel Evart and Yuri's little brother, Piotr.

Cadet Jack Harcourt was one of the "Children of Athena" due to DNA experiments that left his skin color white as cotton. The United Nations passed laws protecting the "Harcourt's" which was their last name given from one of the international criminals involved in the experimentation. All of the rest of the underclassmen and women were also from families that afforded them more "protection" from expulsion than the average cadet and they all knew it.

Gorski's Gang had made plans to celebrate the birthday of Drew Harrison by spending the weekend on Space Station Cy-7.

Harrison had turned 21 years old and his desire was to celebrate with his friends at the Bars, restaurants and shops on Space Station Cy-7. Harrison was the son of an Admiral in the United Nations Space Command who was responsible for an entire Fleet of Space Cruiser space ships. His mother was a diplomatic ambassador that traveled with her husband from solar system to solar system. Drew Harrison's older siblings had already been commissioned as officers in the service. Harrison's father had been African-American from New Jersey. He had been born on a Battle Cruiser and his life as a child had been one of travel across the occupied areas of deep space. As a child, Harrison had been educated in the small schools aboard military space craft and by way of three dimensional broadcasts of lectures from the finest instructors. He learned all of the major subjects such as history, weapons, mathematics, sciences, environmental survival classes, proper operation of cryo-sleep tubes and language studies in which Harrison had become proficient in three languages as was required by United Nations decree. He had stepped on the surface of over thirty planets and about the same number of moons. He was no stranger to dozens of space ships, transports, space stations, floating solar collectors, battle cruisers and asteroid bases. He had seen the far reaches of expansion of humanity.

Drew Harrison was an imposing six foot seven inches tall and his body had solid muscle. He spent most of his spare time lifting weights and participating in aerobic exercise classes. He was studying mechanical engineering, weapons technology and life sciences and maintained good grade points. He was scheduled to graduate with the proper number of collegiate credits.

Harrison had become Gorski's closest friend over the last four years. It was rare to see one without the other. They seemed to have bonded over the years and became as close as brothers.

Harrison had just recently suffered a very bad and public break up with his girlfriend of two years. Her name was Julia Steiner and Harrison had fallen for her at first glance. After a relationship that lasted a few years, Steiner gave him the "Let's see other people" speech. For such a man mountain as he was, his peers would have been surprised to know the pain he felt every time he heard her name, or thought he saw her on campus. Harrison had only confided in Gorski about the deep emptiness he felt from the end of his relationship. Harrison had known he was at risk of losing Steiner when his excessive drinking became an issue with her. Steiner had complained bitterly for months before she ended the association between them.

Harrison arrived at the Docking Bay of the Transport Ship to see the Italian identical twin brothers, Marco and Dominic Andolini, already there. The twins were kicking their ever-present soccer ball back and forth. They were arguing about something in Italian, which they seemed to do all the time. Both of the Andolini's had long dark hair, combed back and straight. They were each 5 foot nine inches tall and had slender builds. Harrison knew that the twin Andolini's had grown up with Gorski, since the age of six. The Andolini's and Gorski were the original members of the group and stood by each other through thick and thin.

Marco and Dominic were identical twins and it was almost impossible to tell them apart with the naked eye. Their parents had decided to build their business on New Edinburgh and left Italy to start their new life. Marco and Dominic had a huge group of siblings, sixteen other brothers and sisters for a total of eighteen in all. Each time their mother gave birth it was to five or six at a time. The parents believed in a large family and frequented medical experts on fertilization to insure a large family. Marco and Dominic were the oldest of the children and were called upon from time to time to supervise the younger offspring. Most of the siblings were sisters and there were three of them that were not quite seventeen years old that gave the brothers fits. The younger sisters were all beautiful and desirable and accordingly attracted much unwanted advances from men. Dominic and Marco had to defend the honor of their three little sisters many times and on some occasions they needed the back up of Gorski and the rest of the Gang.

Harrison was wearing a white sweater with black cargo style pants. His black boots came half way up his legs. He was wearing sun glasses due to his sensitivity to the constant red-orange glow of the New Edinburgh sky.

The new world called New Edinburgh was like Earth in many respects with a similar atmosphere, oxygen, vegetation, large land masses and islands, large water masses, lakes and rivers. There were four main continents that the first human settlers simply named North, East, South and West. The northern continent was approximately the size of North America on Old Earth housed the colonists, the military, the industrial companies, large ranches and the Clovis Academy. The northern continent was about ten percent conquered by humans; the remaining ninety percent was still controlled by the indigenous creatures of the Purple Planet. The other three continents were dominated by the indigenous life forms of New Edinburgh, Triassic and Jurassic style reptiles, felines and insects. Billions of them, large, medium and small and many of them were flesh eaters as the earliest settlers learned the hard way.

Marco Andolini noticed Harrison first. He smiled and tucked the soccer ball under his right arm and rushed to him. He embraced Harrison, "Happy Birthday my friend!"

Dominic followed and hugged Harrison as well. Harrison never understood why the two Andolini's liked to hug everyone all the time. They were clearly both raised to be warm and caring as to others. Marco was studying to be a pilot with minor in weaponry. Dominic had decided to pursue a degree in weaponry and criminal investigations with a minor in tactical skills. Marco was by far the better pilot while Dominic seemed to gravitate more toward weapons proficiency. Dominic was a marksman in several weapons, a great shot with many forms of warfare. At times, Dominic wondered out loud if he should seek to attain a law degree and be a lawyer.

As the three cadets were greeting each other, Yuri Gorski arrived with his latest love interest, Jen Staszko. Gorski stood just a tad over six feet tall and was muscular as he was generally Harrison's weight lifting partner. Gorski had long dark hair with grey-blue eyes and was considered to be very handsome. He was a natural born leader, just as his father was and his mother had been. His major at the Academy was to be an astronaut or a cosmonaut as he would call it. He had wanted to be a pilot since he was a young boy. He was working on his minor in weaponry and criminal investigation. Over the summer break, Gorski had followed in the footsteps of his parents and traveled to old Earth for the Spetsnaz Training. To complete that specialty, one had to survive two months of rigorous survival tests, qualify with high scores on marksmanship, weapon maintenance, several dangerous sky-diving exercises, grueling physical fitness courses and the final exam was a fifty kilometer march, alone, after being dropped in the middle of the Ural mountains and make it back to base. Gorski passed the course while many others failed, and the Spetsnaz training caused several casualties. It was certainly not a challenge for the faint of heart. He had aspired to attend the Spetsnaz course ever since he was a young boy, wanting to make his father proud and to live up to the memory of his long lost mother.

Gorski's current girlfriend was Jen Stasko. She had long, wild, curly cherry blonde hair, brown eyes, and a photogenic face. As a result of what all believed to be her natural beauty, many felt Staszko could have been an actress or super model. Her teeth were perfect. She was a slender five feet ten inches tall, with long, shapely legs, and athletic figure. Not much was known about her past. Staszko claimed her family was gypsies from Eastern Europe on Earth and that she had signed up to come to New Edinburgh because she wanted to leave that life behind. She never really spoke of her family other than that.

Staszko kept her past secret for many reasons. The major justification in her mind was that she had felony charges pending against her on old Earth. Her family had been traveling gypsies, living for the day from town to town, selling entertainment to the locals for money. But, there were many lurking dangers in that life style. One night, Jen Staszko had to defend her aunt in the province that had been known as Bulgaria. Her aunt was being sexually assaulted by a small town chief of police. In an effort to protect her aunt, Staszko stabbed the police chief to death.

Although she acted in defense of another, and probably would have been found not guilty in a trial for the accusation, the local law enforcement wanted her head on a pike. The man she killed had been very popular and from an influential family. There would be no trial and the police were on alert to kill Staszko on sight. In an effort to protect her, Staszko was taken by her family and spirited out of that province to another former nation state. Staszko's family belonged to a network of underground families and was able to transport her to a family doctor, a great uncle. Staszko had been put under the knife, given a new face through the advanced technology in facial reconstruction. She spent a year waiting for her face to heal from the numerous surgeries that her great uncle performed on her behalf. Her doctor had been a very talented man in that Staszko had no scars that would betray her past cosmetic alterations.

After her new face was completed, Staszko's mother and numerous aunts put together enough money to pay for her way to travel to a new planet. She used the money to transport herself to planet New Edinburgh. On her space flight to the strange planet, Staszko studied for her entrance examination for the Academy. She took the formal proficiency test when she arrived on the new unfamiliar world. Staszko passed and was granted entrance as a cadet at the Clovis Academy. To be admitted, Staszko lied on her application on many places, chief among her deceptions was her age. While everyone believed Staszko to be twenty years old, she was really twenty-five. Had she been truthful on her admission paper work, the Academy would not have accepted her. She kept her lies to herself as falsifying a United Nations document was a felony offense. Due to her past life, she always wore knee high boots with sheaths hidden in the interior with throwing knives inside. Although she had not needed to use them in her two years at the Academy, she still carried the weapons, just in case.

Staszko had been with Gorski off and on for the last two years. Many of Academy cadets blamed Staszko for Gorski's break up with Mary Lincoln, his past girlfriend. But that was not accurate and unfair to Staszko as she had not interfered with the relationship between Gorski and Lincoln. She waited until it was officially over before she expressed an interest in being a full time love interest for Gorski.   Staszko knew full well, due to her tough life on old Earth, how difficult it was to find a good man. She had personal experience with bad men, evil men, and corrupt men. Through observation and familiarity, she came to know that Yuri Gorski was a good and decent man and loyal to his friends and family. Those were qualities that were rare in the human experience of the twenty-fifth century. Each day Staszko spent with Gorski was a day she cherished.

The Italian twins hugged Gorski and Staszko upon their arrival.

Gorski shook Harrison's hand, "Happy Birthday my friend!"

Staszko hugged Harrison, "Happy Birthday!" Her accent

was clearly Hungarian; at least that was Harrison's conclusion.

"Thank you my friends," Harrison was smiling at them. "The shuttle transport will be leaving soon. Is anyone else coming along?"

Gorski laughed and handed Harrison a bottle of non-alcoholic Whiskey. "Les and Michel already left and are waiting at the space station for us. The rest will make the later shuttle. For now, the five of us will begin the pre-party."

Harrison took a long sip out of the Whiskey bottle. He coughed as the liquor burned down his throat. "What brand is this?"

Gorski shrugged, "McAmey's Blue Bottle, non-alcoholic. You're favorite as I recall. Nothing but the best." Gorski was always concerned that his dear friend would begin drinking to excess again. Drew Harrison had a problem with alcohol and had abused the substance on several occasions. Harrison would drink to the point of blacking out and not being able to recall the previous night. Accordingly, Gorski would always give Harrison non-alcoholic drinks or attempt to control the amount of drinks he ingested each time the gang went out on the town.

Harrison passed the bottle to Dominic who quickly took a long sip. The Blue Bottle from McAmey's was their premiere brand, costing two-hundred eighty Empire dollars a bottle. The alcohol version cost double that amount. It was a smooth blend of whiskey and could be consumed either straight, over ice or with a mixer. Gorski, as always, had impeccable taste.

As the cadets waited for the signal to board the shuttle, they were bombarded by the three dimensional displays in the sky, all computer generated by nano technology. The programmers and engineers had developed floating micro-chips that were capable of broadcasting large billboard style big screen movies. Advertisements for clothing, restaurants and other various items were in the skies, as if by magic. No sign posts, just floating propaganda to coerce the masses to act in certain ways.

One of the floating advertisements had the image of Pastor Love-Easter, promising eternal life if one was to join his movement. Love-Easter had grown into a very powerful and popular religious leader in the Christian faith. His family was worth millions of Empire Dollars, due to the large amounts of tithing they received. One of his sons, Drayton, rejected the clerical life and joined the Academy on New Edinburgh. Drayton Love-Easter had become one of Yuri Gorski's closest friends.

Each of the three dimensional advertisements would be interrupted by the image of the Earth Empire's Glorious Leader, Secretary General and war hero, Vladimir Sikorsky. He had been the leader for over two hundred years since he led the war against invading aliens on Earth. Sikorsky had rallied the humans in their darkest hour and took the war to the alien home planet. Humanity won under Sikorsky's undaunted leadership and renamed the alien planet Sikorsky's Planet.

Due to the heavy loss of life in that war and the conflicts that followed, Sikorsky initiated a series of laws to increase the human population. He outlawed abortions and contraception. The new government that Sikorsky and his followers created passed additional laws to open adoption orphanages on every planet of the expanding Earth Empire. The children that were not adopted were sent to military camps to be trained as soldiers and on their seventeenth birthday they were ordered into military service. The majority of the enlisted ranks in the Marines, Army, Navy, Space Command and Military Intelligence were former children from the orphan system.

Gorski and his friends watched as the image of the Glorious Leader appeared in the sky. Sikorsky was smiling and looked fantastic for a man that was two hundred forty years old. "My fellow citizens. Remember it is your responsibility to breed and create offspring so that we may spread the seeds of humanity to the furthest reaches of space. Through the children you create by making love, you achieve immortality. I love all of you, my fellow citizens. May the Stars bless you all."

Marco Andolini chuckled. Each time the Glorious Leader promoted sex it guaranteed that he would effortlessly find and bed an attractive woman. Marco and Dominic needed little assistance in that arena as they were famous sports stars on the Clovis City Rattlesnakes. Recently, Dominic had been turning women away without explanation. Marco had speculated that

Dominic was in love with someone and was keeping the relationship secret from the others.

A horn sounded, alerting all passengers to board the shuttle. The group of five cadets loaded on to a transport ship to Space Station Cy-7 at 6:00 p.m. Friday, which was two hours after all classes had ended for the weekend. The transport had a group of eighty civilians and service members all looking to have a great weekend on Space Station Cy-7. Gorski and Staszko loved watching the other citizens whenever they were out and about. They loved to see what others would wear out in public. The current fashion trend seemed to be multi-colored one piece body suits for the men and the women in half shirts and tight shorts with knee high boots.

Lester Brey Gillis, called Les by his friends, was sitting on a three legged stool in the Bar called Tinkerbelle's on Space Station Cy-7. Gillis had been released from class earlier than the majority of the birthday bash attendees so he, along with Michel Darcel Evart, flew ahead of the others to secure several Suites in the luxurious Baroness Hotel. The rooms were expensive, but they were worth it. Gillis was alone as Evart had already met up with a handsome man at the bar and had retired to his room.

Gillis was twenty-one years old, had short red hair, light green eyes, and was about five feet eleven inches tall. He was studying military history and life sciences and was one of the best students at the Clovis Academy. He held a cadet rank of Colonel. After graduation, Gillis planned on transferring to the

Academy on Sikorsky's Planet to study for a Doctorate. Gillis knew that the advanced degree would increase his chances of promotion and duty station requests once he was commissioned. Gillis astounded his professors and friends with his amazing memory, his ability to speak seven languages and discuss past military battles with amazing clarity in the details of the conflicts. He had become a member of Gorski's group when, in his first year at the Academy, he had stood up to Gorski in a fist fight. Gillis did not realize at the time that Gorski was testing his mettle.

Gillis' family was from Cork County, Ireland, and they were all fearless fighters. Gillis had been a boxer and wrestler from a young age, mostly tangling with his older brother, older sisters and cousins. He had also learned to master some of the martial arts and held a black belt. Due to his experiences growing up, Gillis was able to stand up to Gorski and fought him to a standstill.

Gillis had ordered an Irish coffee from the attractive topless waitress. She delivered his drink with a smile. Gillis tipped her well and enjoyed the view. Tinkerbelle's opened its' first bar some fifty years ago and was now a financial success. There were about sixty franchised Tinkerbelle's throughout the Eight Solar Systems. The owners, the Allen family, were already wealthy due to their pioneering in engineering, nuclear energy and their creations that harnessed solar energy. All of the waiters and waitresses at Tinkerbelle's were topless and wore tight shorts and boots. The sign at the entrance of the bar read: *"Tinkerbelle's, where looking is fine, but fondling is encouraged."*

It was well known that this was the bar to go to if you were looking for sex without commitment, regardless of one's orientation. Gillis could see several men meeting one another, women with women and many heterosexual individuals meeting around the bar. Gillis' close friend, Evart, had already had success and took someone up to his room already for a night of romance.

Gillis knew that just a few hundred years ago, people with varying sexual preferences could not interact openly without others judging them harshly. Now, in 2532 The Year of Sikorsky, humanity had grown more accepting and the old biases had gone away with the passing of time.

Gillis had been single for only a few months. He had been with the woman of his dreams, Sophia DuBravac, until he announced his decision to continue his education at the Academy on Sikorsky's Planet. DuBravac was livid at his decision and she put an ultimatum to him. Either me or the extra year at the other Academy, she had demanded. Gillis did not think at the time that DuBravac was serious in her irrational demand, so he chose the Academy and then she walked out of his life. Gillis still loved DuBravac and tried as best he could to get on with his life. Whenever he would see her at the Academy, they would watch each other, with longing in their eyes, but both held too much pride to admit any wrong doing. No words would be shared, only the look of mutual pain for a love lost.

Tinkerbelle's was on the main concourse of the space station, the closest bar to the hotels. It was 18,000 square feet of space for customers to sit and enjoy their time. There was a half-moon cherry wood bar on the wall furthest from the open entrance, with a few dozen chairs around it. The floor had forty-five round tables with the ability to seat three to five people at each table and thirty square tables that could seat up to four people. There were two male bartenders and seven female waitresses working, expecting a heavy crowd as was common on a Friday night. There were holographic pictures of actors, politicians, war heroes and sports stars that had graced Tinkerbelle with their presence over the last three decades.

Gillis looked over the picture of Vladimir Sikorsky, the United Nations Secretary General for the last two hundred twenty years. The Glorious Leader looked great for his age, Gillis thought to himself. Gillis had always wondered how the Glorious Leader had managed to outlive all of the other heroes of the Inter-Planetary Racial Wars. All of the others that had fought the cruel Akarzdamedians had long since passed away except for Sikorsky and his children. Gillis had descended from one of the heroes of that War which was possibly the inspiration from his childhood to study military history. Gillis had written papers on each of the heroes of the Inter-Planetary Racial wars. Gillis had always been disturbed by the mystery surrounding the disappearance of Robert Andrews and his daughters. After the Inter-Planetary Racial Wars had ended, the entire Andrews family vanished from the pages of history.

Gillis spied a group of five women at the far end of the bar, sitting at a round table. They were dressed in professional suits, perhaps office employees. All five were attractive and one of them, an attractive blonde saw Gillis looking in their direction. She gave him a welcome smile. Game on, Gillis thought. He motioned for his waitress to buy the blonde a drink.

The Transport docked with the Space Station after a fifty minute flight. Gorski, Harrison, Staszko and the Andolini twins made their way to the Baroness Hotel and checked in with the automated three dimensional screens. They told the screen their names and placed their hands on the display and their finger prints were recorded. All of the cadets were quickly admitted and carried their luggage up to their rooms. After tossing their luggage, the five met in the lobby and headed to Tinkerbelle's, where their friends were waiting.

The group passed by dozens of civilians and soldiers before they walked briskly into the bar and saw that Gillis was sitting with five women, telling them jokes. The women were all laughing. Gillis had already made points with the blonde, who had introduced herself as Alejandra Khartov. He saw his friends enter the bar and motioned them over. Khartov was sitting in Gillis lap, running her fingers through his hair and occasionally whispering into his ear. Khartov was friendly, outgoing, talkative and clearly enamored with Gillis. As the others approached, Gillis stood to hug his friends. He introduced the five girls to them.

"Les, your friends are handsome. But only three available men? One of my new found friends will be left out," Khartov whispered to Gillis.

Gillis had learned from Khartov that she had just arrived on the space station and wanted to party, so she picked Tinkerbelle's to drink the night away. Khartov struck up a conversation with the other women and they were doing tequila shots when Gillis and Evart had walked in.

Gillis picked Khartov up in his arms and sat down again, sliding her in his lap. "Not to worry, Alejandra. We have more men coming in an hour. Your friends will have plenty to choose from."

Gorski and Staszko cuddled together in a leather couch kissing occasionally and drinking. Harrison had two of the women with Khartov interested in him as he was a physical marvel to behold. The women were asking Harrison to flex his muscles for them. Gorski and Gillis were laughing when Harrison lifted a woman up in each arm. His arm muscles were bulging.

One of the girls told Harrison, "You are amazing. You could change your name to Atlas or Adonis."

CHAPTER THREE

The eight p.m. shuttle arrived a few minutes late on Space Station Cy-7.   April Mejia, a five foot five inch tall twenty year old woman from Santiago, Chile, stepped off the ship and onto the metal floors of the station. She was wearing skin tight jeans, a tube top to accentuate her 38 D-cup breasts, and had her long black hair pulled in a twist tie to the left side of her head. She had on a string of black pearls around her neck. Her knee high black boots made a clacking noise with each step she took on the metallic floor. As she walked, men watched. She was attractive and confident. Mejia was one of the Clovis Academy model students, a good pilot with excellent grades and not one to be toyed with. Although she had a sense of humor, she once broke a man's nose and then his jaw when he made the mistake of grabbing her rear and chest. The man was taken to the surgeons and when he recovered, was never seen around New Edinburgh again.

Mejia had come from a large family and was the first to

leave Earth. Her mother had encouraged her daughter to chase her dreams. Mejia's father was not pleased with her decision to leave and attend the Academy at New Edinburgh. Her brothers and sisters had mixed emotions regarding Mejia's choice. In the end, it was her decision and she left Chile to become an astronaut and an officer in the Space Command. Her father, who had been born in Mexico City, begged her not to go. Although she loved and respected her father, she decided she should take the opportunity to learn to fly space craft.

Behind her was her friend from Corinth, Elektra Papanikolaou. The Greek woman was wearing a white, sleeveless dress with black high heeled shoes. Around her neck, she had on a silver herringbone necklace and matching earrings. She let her long dark hair flow freely. Her white dress had a slit on the left side to show off her legs as she walked. Papanikolaou was tall with piercing green eyes and a slender athletic body. She aspired to work one day in Military Intelligence and was therefore studying military history and security. She was also a fantastic chef, and would cook for the gang Gyros, dolmas, hummus, spanakopita and other cuisine from where she had been raised. She had also come from a large family, as her parents believed in following the laws of the Glorious Leader. Her mother and father would do their duty under the law and breed regularly, producing many children. Her older brothers thought that her leaving to study at the Academy was a great move for her but her sisters were not of the same opinion. Her aunt and uncle had left Earth decades before to attend military academies on the Martian Colonies and Sikorsky's Planet. Her aunt was an Admiral in the naval service and her uncle a Captain in command of his own UnterSee Boot or as the English would refer to as a submarine.

Harumi Shigeta was from Japanese ancestry. She was shorter than the other two women, standing at five feet two inches tall. She moved quickly behind her two friends. Shigeta was wearing a black mini skirt and a skin tight mauve top. She had on a necklace of small silver medallions that dangled just above her breast line. She was nineteen years old and from a family of many that had served in the military. She wanted to be like her older brother, James, and work as a military criminal investigator. She was one of the best criminal justice students at the Academy and very proficient in weaponry. Her older brother kept telling her to study and make the family proud and Shigeta did as instructed. Her grades were in the top ten percent of her class. She held a black belt in ju-jitsu and enjoyed hiking in woodlands. She was also a huge fan of sports, especially soccer, and was able to compete in that sport with the best.

The Rhinehard brothers were next to jump onto the grey metallic floor of the space station. They both wore olive green, long sleeved cadet flight suits. They did not change into civilian clothes since it was well known that women loved pilots and men in uniform. They followed behind their three female friends. Klaus Rhinehard was the oldest at twenty and his brother, Rolf, was nineteen. The two brothers moved fast, to keep pace with the three girls and join the birthday party at Tinkerbelle's for Drew Harrison.

Klaus had been in lust for April Mejia for the past year. It had been love at first sight for him. The memory of when he first saw her would forever be in his mind. He watched her walk in front of him. Klaus could never get Mejia to pay attention to him, no matter how hard he tried. Their interactions had been as fellow cadet astronauts and nothing more.

Both Klaus and Rolf were from Dresden, Germany on old Earth. They had blonde hair, blue eyes and chiseled, muscular bodies. Rolf was the tallest at six feet and Klaus just an inch shorter.

Klaus had watched the many space ship launches from Dresden as a child. His father and mother encouraged him in his dream to be a space ship pilot. He payed special attention in his science and mathematics classes so he could one day qualify for the honor of attending a Space Command Academy. He studied and studied. He achieved high grades and was accepted into the Clovis Academy. In his first week as a cadet, he had his run in with some bullies, the infamous Farinelli brothers, after class. Klaus had been raised to fight back and on that day he did just that. He fought seven all by himself. He took a beating before Yuri Gorski, Drew Harrison, Les Gillis and Drayton Love-Easter intervened. The seven abusive cadets, members of a group known as the Bragg Gang, were left defeated and flattened on the concrete landing strip. Due to his willingness to stand and fight, Klaus was invited by Gorski to join the Gang. Understanding the concept of strength in numbers, Klaus readily accepted the kind request and became a member.

The next year, when younger brother Rolf joined the Academy, he was accepted by Gorski and the others without question. Klaus vouched for his little brother, and the younger Rhinehard held his own in each bar fight that they were a part of. Rolf was a womanizer and had a drive to break up couples by stealing the girl away from another man. That propensity on the part of Rolf would obviously start many fights. Yuri Gorski had to admonish the younger Rhinehard on many occasions regarding his behavior. Gorski had never expelled anyone from the gang, but Rolf had the potential of being the first if he did not change his ways.

Dirk Fenster and Archibald Frazier were the next two members of the gang to exit the Transport ship. They moved quickly as the party was already two hours underway. Fenster and Frazier were eighteen year old cadets that shared the same dormitory room. Fenster was from one of the wealthiest families in the entire United Nations of Earth. Frazier had come from a middle class family. The two cadets were randomly assigned by the administration to share the same quarters at the Academy. Frazier and Fenster became friends quickly when Frazier came to Fenster's defense during an incident of hazing by an upper class man. Both Frazier and Fenster had dark hair and were both about five feet eleven inches tall. Fenster was studying to be a pilot, although he already knew how to fly any form of space craft since his family probably either built them or designed them or both. Frazier was fascinated by geology and was studying to become an explorations officer. They were an odd set of friends, Fenster wealthy beyond imagination and Frazier from humble beginnings. Within a few days on campus, Fenster and Frazier had both observed that there were many student gangs at the Academy. They were astute enough to recognize that it was best practice to have someone watching your back at all times. Many cadets were cruel and even sadistic, mercilessly hazing other students. It was especially risky for the cadets that were the loners and failed to align themselves with any group. Frazier and Fenster were intended victims in one such sudden aggressive action. On their fifth day at the Academy, Frazier and Fenster were jumped by members of the Bragg Gang. Fenster and Frazier stood back to back, swinging away at the Bragg brothers. Unknown to Fenster and Frazier, Love-Easter and Gillis were watching the fist fight from a distance. At one point, Love-Easter and Gillis intervened and came between Frazier and Fenster and the Bragg Gang. Fenster watched as Gillis and Love-Easter took on nine aggressors and beat them all. Soon after that day, Gillis and Love-Easter presented Frazier and Fenster to Gorski and advocated that they should be admitted to the Gorski Gang. Frazier and Fenster were grateful to be included into the group as membership in any gang would end hazing incidents and provide protection in numbers.

Cadet Drayton Love-Easter was next to step onto the metal floor of the space station docking bay. He was a buff five foot nine inches tall with blonde hair and light brown eyes. He was the oldest son of Pastor Jonathan Love-Easter who was the most popular "Broadcast Evangelist" in the Eight Solar Systems. His father was very charismatic and had convinced about fifty million people to tattoo the symbol of the cross on their faces as a show of their faith. Instead of following his fathers' footsteps into the ministry, Drayton had wanted to see the Universe. He immediately left Earth when Clovis Academy accepted him as a cadet. Last summer, he and Yuri Gorski were the only two Clovis Academy Cadets to be selected to attend the elite Spetsnaz training. They attended the Spetsnaz course with eighty highly qualified cadets and only forty-one had completed the process, including Gorski and Love-Easter.

Love-Easter had several younger siblings that he would keep in contact with via Three-Dimensional Broadcast chat rooms. Since he had rejected the life of a man of the cloth, his father wanted nothing to do with him. He had not spoken to his father in over three years, even though he had made several attempts. His mother kept telling him to give his father time to accept his career choice decision.

Since leaving his family, Love-Easter had accomplished many of his goals. He was scheduled to graduate with his class in May. He had completed the grueling Spetsnaz instruction and was one of the best marksmen in the Academy. Although he had achieved many milestones, he lived with many regrets. One was that his father had disowned him for turning his back on the family church. The second was Love-Easter's most painful. As an entering cadet, he had found love with a lovely and caring woman named Yesenia Guevara, who had been a fellow Gorski Gang member and currently a fellow cadet at the Academy. During their relationship, he fathered a child with the woman. His hope was to marry Guevara and spend his life with her and his child. Unfortunately, another cadet named Melissa Harcourt, a Child of Athena, had used her genetically altered powerful scents to lure Love-Easter to her bed. While he was in the throes of passion with Harcourt, Guevara caught them together. Love-Easter did not realize that was just what Harcourt had planned. Feeling betrayed, Guevara ended the relationship and left Love-Easter forever. Although he begged her on numerous occasions to come back to him, Guevara would not forgive him. In an effort to avoid losing her child to mandatory adoption laws, Guevara married another cadet. The man that Guevara married had been a member of a rival group to the Gorski Gang. Love-Easter believed that Guevara had chosen her husband as a way to get revenge on him. Love-Easter had never been able to forgive himself and he despised Melissa Harcourt for using him in the manner she had. The Children of Athena were irresistible when they used their aromas or mind control powers on another person. If a Child of Athena targeted another for physical sex, the object of the Child of Athena would be powerless to resist.

Last off of the transport was twenty year old Jack Harcourt. Jack was a cadet pilot at the Academy from a planet named Athena. All of the Children of Athena had the surname Harcourt. They were children from Athena that were the product of an experiment in which thousands of women were forced to participate in under threat of death. About forty-five years earlier, a medical Doctor named Raquel Church living on the Earth-like planet Athena had taken the sperm of the military commander of her colony, Colonel Simon Harcourt, and fertilized the eggs of the women forced into the procedure. The fertilized eggs were frozen for implantation in women that were scheduled to arrive at the colony on later dates. Colonel Harcourt and Doctor Church had every woman on Athena impregnated; even women just passing through on business or tourists. No woman was exempt from their mad experiment. Any woman of child bearing age that resisted was arrested and impregnated by force. Thousands of children were born from this procedure. Over time it was discovered that many of the off-spring developed several defects. The most recognizable trait of the children of the medical experiment was that all of them were born with skin as white as snow. Doctor Church never attempted to discover the medical reason for that mutation. The offspring were named the "Children of Athena."

Jack Harcourt was a second generation Child of Athena, which meant he had developed additional mutations. One such genetic variance was their ability to emit seductive odors or a pleasant smell to attract a mate. The humans that were attracted by the pleasant smells would find the Harcourt suitor irresistible. Another second generation Child of Athena difference was the ability to read minds. The capacity to read minds ranged from the skill to sense a person's emotions to the higher level talent to predict a person's movement before the act occurred. He developed the power to take over another person's mind, manipulate and control their actions.   Some of the Harcourt's had been rumored to have other abilities that Jack Harcourt never attempted to access such as telekinesis, seeing the future and other abilities.

Jack was unwilling to use his gifts or powers. He knew that he could cause emotional damage by luring women to his bed for his pleasure. He had also been lucky enough to learn as a young man that entering the mind of another without permission was a vile act. It was akin to a physical violation only it was done so mentally. Jack was too verecund in his personality to attempt such acts.

Due to the abilities from the mutations, Jack Harcourt had to endure odd stares from strangers and sometimes even physical attacks. When he received the request from Yuri Gorski to join the little band of cadets, he did not hesitate and became a member without question.

The creators of the Children of Athena, Colonel Harcourt and Doctor Church, had fled over thirty-five years ago to escape indictment and prosecution for civil rights violations. They were never arrested and their fate remained one of the great mysteries of the Eight Solar Systems.

The group of cadets led by Mejia moved quickly toward the bar named Tinkerbelle's to rendezvous with Gorski, Harrison and the others.

Unseen by the cadets were three young men that watched the women go by. The three men were standing in the main walk way of the space station, looking over each and every person from the Docking Bay. Two of the men were the sons of the wealthiest and most powerful men on planet New Edinburgh known as Alfred Rosenburg, II. One was named Caine Rosenburg and his younger half-sibling was Darryl Rosenburg.

The third man was Caine's friend, Avery "Big Bad" Jackson. Caine and Jackson were students at the Achilles Academy located on another planet called New Quebec in the same solar system as Sikorsky's Planet. Caine had brought a few of his Academy friends to meet his father, uncle and his vast number of siblings and cousins due to the week long holiday on planet New Quebec celebrating her conquest two hundred years back. Caine had forty-nine siblings, at least that he was aware of. His father had several wives and many more women on the side. Caine's father was a lecherous man and Caine hoped to grow up to have just as many lovers and children. Caine idolized his father and some of his older brothers. Caine had long dark hair, parted in the middle, blue eyes and stood about six foot tall. He was only in the Achilles Academy to please his father. All of the members of the Rosenburg clan were expected to become engineers, lawyers, doctors, military heroes so that each could build a resume worthy of selection into governmental service. Caine was scheduled to graduate at the end of the year and go on to medical school as some of his brothers and sisters had done. He intended to be successful and make his father proud.

Caine had been a killer since his early teenage years. At the age of thirteen he had been taken to one of the slave houses on the Rosenburg Ranch Territory by his brother Cush. As the owners of all of the slaves, the Rosenburg's could do as they wished with them. Caine found himself an attractive blonde woman, a bit older than he had been at the time, and took her to his room. Caine had taken a hit of some Red Dust which was a hyper-potent psychedelic synthetic drug. While under the influence of the Red Dust, all of his senses were heightened. Making love to the slave woman was one of his greatest experiences in life; murdering her felt even better. Although the woman was compliant and performed all of the sex acts that Caine demanded, he murdered her anyway. He felt compelled to stab the lovely woman after enjoying having sex with her. Using a steak knife that he had carried with him, he began to slash the woman repeatedly. He committed the violent murder because he wanted to be just like his father. He had watched his father kill slave women many times over the years. Caine emulated his father and even drank the dying woman's blood as he had seen his father do with past victims. He recalled that he walked out into the large hall of the slave house, nude and covered in blood. The sight of the bloody young lad was shocking to those in the room. Brother Cush never invited young Caine to any further outings.

Caine did not let the disappointment of Cush dissuade his insatiable desire to hear the screams of someone that was begging for their lives. Caine began a career as a stalker. He longed for the time he could spend locating lovely women, follow them for months and learn all he could about them. And when the time was right, he would butcher his target to death. Some of the women he would rape first, others he did not, and it just depended on his mood at the time. When Caine left planet New Edinburgh to attend the Academy at another planet, he laid low for a few months until he decided his female Professor in Military History should be his next victim. Her body parts were never found by the law enforcement officers investigating her case. Caine still had the Professor's eye in a safe jar full of a liquid solution to maintain his prize and remind him of the thrill of the kill.

Caine's half-sibling, eighteen year old Darryl, had the same physical features and height. Darryl idolized his older sibling and would follow him everywhere, almost like his shadow. Caine had never included Darryl in any of his past illicit actions. Caine had told Darryl several times about the thrill of locating an unsuspecting victim, hunting them down, violating, torturing and ultimately killing them. Caine enjoyed showing Darryl the mementoes of each of his victims. A finger, an ear, a nose and several eyes that would remind Caine of the past thrill of the hunt. To Caine, the joy of taking a life was not in the act of murder itself, but the selection of the victim and stalking them.

Darryl would listen to his brother tell the tales of past victims. Darryl had begged Caine to include him and to allow him to participate in the hunt. Caine finally relented and agreed to include Darryl in the next bind, torture and kill session.

The Rosenburg siblings had been raised in a culture that did not respect life. Their father had built a large Arena in the center of the Rosenburg Ranch Territory of planet New Edinburgh in which many died. Caine and Darryl had witnessed men and women die at the hands of other humans. They had also been present to see humans eaten to death by large carnivores. They had found that there were thousands of ways to kill another human being. Although they had seen others murdered, Caine was cognizant of the fact that Darryl had never actually killed a person before. Accordingly, their targets for rape and torture had to be easy marks. The killing event had to be controlled so that his brother Darryl would not be able to make a fatal mistake for himself.

Caine's friend, Avery Jackson, had earned the nickname of "Big Bad" at the Achilles Academy. He was almost seven feet tall, sporting bulging muscles, black skin, yellow eyes and his smile revealed a small gap between his two front upper teeth. Like Caine, Jackson was also in his last year at the Academy. Jackson was not a scholastic success as he barely passed his classes. Jackson had been born to vain parents that wanted "super-children" and his parents paid considerable sums of Empire Dollars to achieve their desires. While Jackson's mother was pregnant, her Doctor's injected the fetus with DNA strains from several wild kingdom animals. The procedure had been medically approved for over a hundred years. The genetic alteration procedures made Jackson stronger, faster and more agile than the average human. Caine recognized immediately that Jackson was a person that would be useful to him. He had hired Jackson to stay with him as a paid body guard almost every day.

Caine learned that Jackson had killed at least seven people and had raped and murdered a fourteen year old girl. Caine paid off police, judges, politicians and prosecutors to make the evidence disappear and have the charges dismissed. Due to the protection Caine had given to Jackson, he was in is debt many times over. One of the murders committed by Jackson was at Caine's request. There was a female student at the Academy that refused to sleep with Caine, so he and Jackson broke into her dormitory room late at night and, after brutally raping the girl, Caine watched with glee as Jackson hacked her to pieces with a machete.

Jackson once told Caine a chilling story of his past. When Jackson was just eleven years old, he had lived in a decent residential area on Earth. There was a large community swimming pool that Jackson and his family would go to on the weekends and holidays. There was a young girl that Jackson had a crush on. He told Caine that one day, he pinched the girl on her bottom at the swimming pool. The girl cried and told her parents on Jackson. Jackson recalled his father delivering a beating on him which left scars on his back. He waited for about six or seven months for his chance at revenge on the little girl that had gotten him into trouble. Jackson saw her one day at school while she was alone on the playground. Jackson told Caine he walked up to the girl and wrapped his hands around her throat and strangled her to death. Jackson left her dead body on a swing. He was never arrested or charged for that murder as there had been no witnesses to the incident. He told Caine that he never felt so alive than he did when he saw the look in that little girl's eyes as he strangled her. Jackson related that seeing the look in the eyes of a dying person was better than sex.

"Which one do you like?" Caine asked as the women walked past them.

Jackson licked his lips watching Mejia walk by him, focusing on her breasts, "I like the short Latina. I want her. And you?"

Caine smiled as he pointed his Holo-com device in the direction of the women to capture their images, "I want the tall brunette in the white dress. How about you little brother?"

Darryl watched the women and shrugged. "I agree with Avery. The short one is hot. Will I really get to have sex with her?"

Caine nodded, "Better than just sex. We'll hold her down for you and then we'll let you help us cut her up."

"And if they resist?" Darryl asked.

Caine shrugged, "We'll use them and hack them to pieces regardless. No one tells us 'No'." Caine motioned to the long hallway leading away from the Docking Bay. "Come on, let's round up the others. I think Lomax and Chin are at their rooms in the Slatkin Inn. We need to match their images to the computer data base and get names to go along with the faces."

Jackson followed Caine obediently. He cared little that Caine was a psychotic serial rapist and murderer. Jackson held others in contempt and had little value for the lives of others, so he enjoyed his fellowship with Caine as the two men found mutual pleasure in taking innocent lives. For Jackson the pleasure was doubled because Caine paid him to assist in the kill. Darryl followed as well, excited that he was finally being accepted by his older brother.

CHAPTER FOUR

The party at Tinkerbelle's was in full swing when Mejia and the others walked in. The Andolini brothers gave hugs of welcome to the rest of their gang. Gillis and Alejandra Khartov had already decided to take their leave and said their good byes leaving to spend the rest of the evening together in Gillis' hotel room. Gorski greeted each of his friends. Everyone gave birthday wishes to Drew Harrison and started buying him shots of whiskey or tequila. Harrison was already under the influence after several rounds of toasts to his birthday. Gorski shook his head "no" when asked if there should be another round of liquor shots for Harrison. Gorski felt his friend had too much to drink already.

Papanikolaou and Mejia walked straight for the bar. Frazier and Fenster followed them. Frazier had a huge crush on the tall Greek woman which started the first time he tasted her cooking. His infatuation with her grew over the months and the more he got to know her, the more he liked her.

The two young men listened to the women asking the handsome bartender about the drink specials, suddenly Papanikolaou gasped, pointing at the row of wine bottles behind the half-moon bar.

"Is that Mavrodaphne?" Papanikolaou asked.

The bartender nodded, "Yes ma'am. We import that wine in from Greece. It's three hundred Empire Dollars a bottle."

Papanikolaou looked down at her feet, clearly disappointed. "That's kind of expensive. When I lived in Greece those bottles would have been no more than thirty."

The bartender shrugged, "Import fees. It's really expensive to ship across several star systems. You understand."

She nodded, "I haven't had a glass in almost two years."

Fenster, sensing this was Frazier's moment, slipped a thousand Empire Dollars into his hand, "Pretend this is your money and buy her a bottle."

Frazier looked at the money in his hand and counted it. "Dirk, are you sure? That is a lot of money."

Fenster shrugged off the statement. Frazier was a good friend and Fenster wanted to give him an assist in his desire to get to know Elektra better. "Arch, I get ten times this every month for my allowance. Take the money and impress the girl. Besides, she always cooks those delicious Greek meals for us at the dormitory. It's about time we all did something for her. Buy her the bottle. Buy two. Do it for her and do it for yourself."

Frazier thanked him and turned to the bartender, "Sir, can I buy the lady one of those wine bottles?"

Papanikolaou turned to Frazier and seemed surprised. He smiled at her. "As long as you don't mind sharing a glass with me."

Papanikolaou walked over to Frazier as he paid the bartender the three hundred dollar fee. "Thank you Arch. That is very sweet of you."

The bartender delivered the bottle after removing the cork and two glasses. Frazier poured the wine. "Why don't we grab a seat over there and enjoy the wine together?"

Papanikolaou smiled and took a sip from her glass. The flavor was better than she had remembered. She closed her eyes, savoring the taste, the feel of the wine rushing down her throat. It felt warm. She realized Frazier was being more than just kind. He was making an obvious pass at her. She looked at his face, thinking that he was very handsome. She had always liked the way his thick eye brows and piercing eyes looked. Why not, she asked herself. "Yes, let's do that."   The two found a couch and sat down next to each other enjoying the wine.

Drayton Love-Easter located an empty chair and pulled it next to Gorski and Staszko. He noticed that the Andolini brothers were flirting with the girls Gillis had introduced them to. Harrison was also conversing with the women, having the full attention of two of them. Gillis had ordered a food tray from the waitress and was sharing with the group before he left the party with Khartov. Marco was eating slices of sharp cheddar cheese on wheat wafers. Harrison was sampling the fried Disavra Sticks, a white fish from the oceans of planet New Edinburgh that was delicious.

Love-Easter raised his glass of Whiskey and cola, "Here's to Spetsnaz."

Gorski clanked his glass with Love-Easter's. They drank. "I thought you were going to be on the same shuttle with us. What happened to you?" Gorski wanted to know.

"I had an appointment that ran a little later than I had thought," Love-Easter told him. He leaned in close to Gorski and Staszko. "I scored some pot, come by room later and we can get high. It's from the virgin forest farmers on New Edinburgh. The best quality from Lynott's province."

Staszko, who was in Gorski's lap, purred, "Mmmmmm, that does sound good. What do you think, Yuri? It's legal. Not like its' Red Dust, Synthetic Vertigo or Hydro-Cocaine or some other outlawed substance. And, we are over eighteen...."

Gorski shrugged at the suggestion. His only fear was if his father found out that he used any drug, legal or not. His father was a typical strict Marine Corps officer and made certain that his sons did not engage in activities that might harm their future. But up on the Space Station, the chances of his father finding out were slim. "Sure, why not? Like you said, Jen, it is legal."

Marijuana had been legalized by the United Nations for use by anyone eighteen or older in 2111, A.D. The government controlled the growing, packaging, distribution and sales of the formerly illegal drug and used the profits to fund the purchase of more militarized space craft. The drug cartels of the time fought the legalization movement and there were several drug cartel related assassinations. The government military fought back. But, in the end, the United Nations prevailed. The drug cartels were financially damaged by the short war. Now, the cartels produced more potent drugs to profit off of. The current government enforced the drug laws as an afterthought with no major law enforcement effort to specialize in drug enforcement. It was rumored that the cartels paid tributes to the controlling Sikorsky family to "look the other way" and not enforce the drug laws. Other rumors suggested that the cartels and the government were in partnership. Whatever the reason, purchasing illegal substances was relatively a risk free act.

Staszko pointed to another table with three attractive women and two men. The five were staring over at them. "Dray, looks like you have some fans over there."

Love-Easter looked over and saw the five strangers. They all had the cross tattooed on their left cheeks. Love-Easter sighed. "I bet they have seen my picture from my family portraits on dad's religious broadcasts. Everywhere I go, someone knows who I am."

"Sucks to be you," Gorski was laughing. "I think they

want to talk to you. Maybe get your autograph?"

Love-Easter grunted, "Perhaps I should take the blonde on the left and ask her if she wants to procreate."

Staszko laughed. Her favorite quality in Love-Easter had been his warped sense of humor. He always seemed to have something to say to lighten them moment. "She won't find that offensive? I thought sex was not allowed in the religion unless you were married."

"Not when I point out that the first Commandment to Adam and Eve was to be fruitful and multiply," Love-Easter said standing up. Both Gorski and Staszko were laughing. "Come by later, hopefully I will not be alone."

"We will be there," Gorski said as Love-Easter walked over to the five strangers. He shook hands with them and sat down next to the blonde that he had pointed out.

April Mejia and Harumi Shigeta had met two male pilots from the U.N.S.C. *Colorado*, a science vessel that was in orbit around New Edinburgh. The two pilots were on "R and R" leave, Rest and Relaxation, for the weekend and had been to some of the Tinkerbelle Bars at other Cy Space Stations. One of the pilots was a Lieutenant, his name tag read Jahn and the other was a Lieutenant Commander named Ilyasova. The pilots approached the two girls, bought them a round of drinks and the conversation began.

The girls learned that the *Colorado* was ordered to survey the outer areas of space, searching asteroids for valuable iron, tungsten, titanium, cobalt and other heavy metals by using long range photographic technology. Mejia kept catching the two men staring at her breasts. She began second guessing her decision to wear the skin tight tube top. She was clearly getting the wrong kind of attention. Shigeta also noticed that the two men were spending most of the eye contact on Mejia's ample bust.

Mejia finally said, "Hey pinche bolillo, my eyes are up here."

The two men seemed a bit embarrassed. Ilyasova apologized to her and they continued the conversation, trying not to let their eyes wander. Jahn did not speak much, allowing his superior officer to do most of the talking. Ilyasova bought another round of drinks and ordered a round of shots. Shigeta knew that the men were trying to get the girls drunk so they could get them to their rooms.

Mejia told the pilots that she was studying to be a pilot and would be graduating from the Academy the year after this one. Ilyasova suggested that the girls join them on board the Raumschiff and perhaps Mejia could fly the ship. No one would know that they violated regulations. It would be their little secret, Ilyasova assured them. Another Lieutenant approached them, his name tag read Griffin, and his uniform patches were the same as Ilyasova and Jahn. They shook hands, and introduced Griffin to Shigeta and Mejia. Griffin also was focusing on Mejia's chest. Shigeta felt she had enough of the three fly boys and politely excused herself to the ladies room. The majority of the pilots Shigeta had met were arrogant, self-centered and they acted as if every woman should sleep with them. Shigeta could tell these three from the U.N.S.C. *Colorado* were of the same personality. Shigeta had wanted to spend an evening having fun, not wasting the night away listening to three fly boys going on and on about how great they are. Shigeta motioned slightly with her head to Mejia to follow her, but she stayed with the three officers. She speculated in her mind that her friend really wanted to fly the ship as Ilyasova promised her.

As Shigeta walked away, Ilyasova motioned to an open "U" shaped booth near the far left wall. He took Mejia by her hand and led her to the booth. She followed him and sat down. Ilyasova sat next to her on her right and Griffin to her left. Jahn sat next to Griffin. Ilyasova was flirting with Mejia, and soon had his hand on her shapely leg.

Shigeta walked up to Fenster and the Rhinehard brothers who were looking out the back observation bay windows behind the back of Tinkerbelle's. The three cadets were drinking schnapps and speaking of the day that they would get to pilot all of the ships docked to the space station.

"Having fun?" Shigeta asked them.

Fenster poured a drink of schnapps into an empty glass, passed it to her and nodded. "Better now, with you here."

Shigeta took the drink from him and raised her left

eyebrow. "Why better?"

"Because you are the most attractive lady in the house. And, now, you are here with us," Fenster said before gulping down a mouth full of schnapps.

Shigeta laughed out loud. "You must be drunk. My friend April is the pretty one. Those three fly boys sure want a piece of her."

Fenster nodded, digging his elbow into Klaus Rhinehard's ribs. "We noticed. Does she need us to get her out of there?" Fenster knew of the elder Rhinehard's desires toward Mejia. Fenster had encouraged Klaus to tell Mejia how he felt and let her know of his interest. For some reason, Klaus was too shy. Perhaps he was afraid of being rejected, Fenster thought to himself.

Shigeta shrugged, "They promised her that they were going to let her fly their ship. April seemed impressed by that." Shigeta looked back at her friend with a look of concern. Mejia had finished another shot, and was starting to get drunk. All three men were back to undressing Mejia with their eyes. "She may not like it, but I think intervention could be a good idea. Those fly boys are up to no good." Shigeta noticed that Klaus was watching the three officers and he seemed to be jealous. Shigeta had never caught on that Klaus had any attraction to Mejia. Shigeta knew that Mejia did not like to get involved with any of the men in the group, but Mejia had confided in her on several occasions that the exception would be Klaus.

Rolf finished his drink and gave the glass to Fenster to pour him another. "Those three officers are starting to get really friendly with April. Are they all three planning on taking her to the ship? Three on one? April is more adventurous than I thought."

The comment elicited dirty looks from Klaus and Shigeta. Fenster had learned from past experience to ignore Rolf's inappropriate comments.

Shigeta saw that Griffin and Ilyasova would touch Mejia's arm, put their arms around her waist, and touch her bare shoulders. Mejia was laughing at some joke Ilyasova was telling her and she seemed oblivious to the touches.

Shigeta looked at the three cadets, "I think we should watch it just in case we have to get her out of there." As she was speaking, Ilyasova had pulled Mejia into his lap. Mejia seemed cuddle in the Lieutenant Commander's embrace willingly. Shigeta could tell that Mejia was attracted to Ilyasova so she concluded that as for now, Mejia was doing exactly as she wanted.

Shigeta continued to drink with the three men, every now and then looking over her shoulder to check on Mejia. Shigeta saw Ilyasova massaging Mejia's shoulders. Mejia was smiling, so Shigeta thought nothing of it. It was not the first time Mejia met a man at a bar and left with him for sex. Shigeta could tell by Mejia's demeanor and body language that she liked Ilyasova.

"Your skin feels so soft," Ilyasova whispered into Mejia's ear.

Mejia looked over her shoulder at Ilyasova, "Thank you."

Mejia saw Griffin and Jahn watching their senior officer, as if they wanted to be the ones with Mejia in their lap. She thought that their behavior was odd given all the other single and available women in the bar.

Mejia believed that she was not in any peril. These were officers and they were in a public place. Nothing bad would happen. Ilyasova was just getting a little too friendly, that was all. Besides, Mejia was very much attracted to Ilyasova and she had already decided she wanted to go back to his ship sleep with him. He was muscular, handsome, and very bold. She felt his hands running up and down her back.

"You are very beautiful," Ilyasova told her.

Mejia thanked him, with a lack of anything else to say. She could feel that Ilyasova was getting aroused. Soon want to take her to his hotel room, or his ship. Mejia knew when a man desired her and this man really wanted her, lusted for her. She knew he would suggest that they leave together and she would politely tell her friends some lame excuse and leave with him. To Mejia's surprise, Ilyasova turned out to be far more forward and aggressive than she was used to.

Ilyasova, emboldened by Mejia's lack of resistance, slid his hands around her waist and kissed her playfully on her neck.

Mejia smiled and thought, okay, let's go to your room. She wanted to suggest it, but felt the man should be the one to initiate the request. While Ilyasova had his hands around her waist, Mejia felt his fingers brush over her breasts, as if it were not intentional by the man. He would reach across her, take a drink, and when he would return his hand around her he would brush over chest. Ilyasova would kiss Mejia on her neck and shoulders occasionally as he played his little game of touch with her.

Ilyasova grew even bolder when he moved his hands upwards settling around her chest. She felt his palms and fingers softly massaging her breasts. She looked down, stunned that she was being fondled by the pilot in public. Mejia was shocked that a Lieutenant Commander, an officer in the Space Command, was actually feeling her out in a location with hundreds of witnesses. Mejia had never believed that an officer would attempt that with her in a public place, especially while he was in uniform. The Military Code had rules against such behavior. Stunned by his actions she began thinking of a way to get away from the man as his hands cupping her breasts, fondling them for all to see.

Ilyasova continued to enjoy feeling out Mejia's chest whispered into her ear, "You have a remarkable body."

Mejia, embarrassed that she was being touched in such a manner in public, did not really know what to say. She decided to get away from Ilyasova before things got too intense.

Mejia cleared her throat and told the Lieutenant Commander, "I think I need to go to the ladies room. I will be right back."

Mejia attempted to stand up but Ilyasova held her chest tightly and did not allow her to leave. Mejia then concluded that she may well be in peril. She felt Ilyasova slide his hands underneath her tube top and pull it upwards. Now, his hands were on her bare breasts.

Mejia could see Jahn and Griffin enjoying the view.

"Hey cabron, cuidate con los manos!" Mejia blurted out.

"What did you say sweet tits?" Griffin laughed at her. "I did not understand a word you said."

"I said to watch it with the hands!" Mejia was wriggling in Ilyasova's arms attempting to leave. He held her tight so she could not escape from him.

Since Mejia was on Ilyasova's lap, she could feel the pilot was now completely aroused. He turned her toward him and kissed her on the lips. Mejia thought that this man was going to have sex with her right there in front of everyone. Griffin and Jahn were watching every second of what was occurring, voyeurs without a doubt.

Ilyasova asked Mejia if she would mind letting his two friends join in. Mejia shook her head and said, "No. This needs to stop. You are out of line!"

Ilyasova laughed and motioned to his two friends with his head to move in closer. Mejia slapped Ilyasova on his left cheek which only angered the pilot. He grabbed her by the wrists and held her arms up high as Griffin slid over next to them on the booth and began fondling her breasts from behind her. Jahn moved Griffin aside and told him he wanted to join in. Mejia struggled but Ilyasova held her arms tight as Jahn's hands softly cupped her large breasts. Mejia's face was inches from Ilyasova's and she could see his smile as he laughed at her. Mejia heard Jahn ask her if he could kiss her tits, or something vulgar along those lines.

Before she could answer him, she heard Klaus Rhinehard's voice.

"There you are, mein liebchen!" Klaus came up to her and forcefully pushed Ilyasova aside with his left hand. Klaus took hold of her arms and pulled her toward him. He hugged her close and pulled her tube top back down over her chest. He could feel Mejia shivering, most likely from fear or anger or both. Klaus put his blue flight jacket over her shoulders. Mejia was relieved that he had come to her rescue.

Ilyasova stood up angry, his face was red and he was grinding his teeth. He did not appreciate being shoved and certainly not from a punk cadet. Ilyasova had grown up in an orphanage on the Martian Colonies and had learned to fight at an early age. In fact, he had been exposed to an environment that instilled in him the necessity to fight first and negotiate later. "Who the hell are you?"

"I'm her boyfriend!" Klaus responded sternly and then to Mejia he said softly, "Come on. Let's go."

Klaus put his arm around Mejia's shoulders in a protective manner and turned his back on Ilyasova and began walking Mejia back toward Shigeta, Fenster and Rolf. Then, without warning, Jahn grabbed Klaus by his left shoulder, spun him around and punched him in the face. Klaus went down hard to the floor and was flat on his back. He felt blood on his chin as the jab from Jahn had split his lower lip. Mejia turned and kicked Jahn in the groin. Jahn fell to his knees, cupping his privates in his hands, crying out in pain. Fenster and Rolf witnessed the cowardly attack on Klaus. They both rushed in and began throwing wild punches at Ilyasova and Griffin. Mejia and Shigeta helped Klaus to his feet.

As if from nowhere, other pilots, repair technicians and computer operatives from the United Nations Space Command Cruiser *Colorado* joined in the brawl. Fenster and Rolf were overwhelmed by the sheer strength in numbers. Fenster was picked up by some seven foot tall technician and thrown on top of a bar table, which collapsed under the impact. Fenster yelled out a four letter expletive just before the forced contact onto the table. Rolf was able to get in two good punches on Ilyasova before someone slammed the young cadet over his back with a bar stool. The younger Rhinehard fell to his knees, the world was spinning.

The employees of Tinkerbelle's staff ran behind the bar for cover. That reaction was standard operating procedure to protect themselves in the event of violence in the bar. The innocent patrons began rushing out the front entrance or hid under tables. One older, well dressed, businessman stood up, watching the fight and was laughing as people went down.

Jack Harcourt had been flirting with one of the waitresses when Klaus was knocked to the ground. He politely excused himself from the bar employee and jumped into the fray. Harcourt punched one *Colorado* technician in the nose before he was grabbed by three men in black Military Intelligence uniforms. All three of the men had the symbol of the U.N.S.C. *Colorado* on their shoulders and had enlisted stripes on their collars. Two of them held Harcourt's arms while the third began punching Harcourt in the stomach and face. By the looks on their faces, they were enjoying the chance to beat a Harcourt.

Klaus, Mejia and Shigeta began fighting back against three to one odds.

Mejia was angrier than she had ever been in her life. She was beside herself in that these idiots would all support Ilyasova treating her in such a manner in front of everyone. Mejia kicked one man in the groin, which sent him to the floor and then she kicked him in the face. Blood spattered out of the man's mouth. "Puto!" Mejia screamed at him.

Shigeta had spun around Mejia and drop kicked one technician in the chest sending him staggering backwards into the bar. She hit a charging woman in a technician uniform under her jaw and the woman flipped backwards and landed hard on the floor.

Gorski and Staszko saw the man that Shigeta had kicked fall backwards into the bar area. Staszko stood up from his lap and pointed at the commotion on the other side of the establishment. "Yuri! Our Gang is getting whipped!"

"Move it!" Gorski yelled in the direction of Dominic and Marco when he stood next to Staszko and noticed his friends were under attack.

Frazier and Papanikolaou were sitting together on a couch, enjoying their second bottle of Mavrodaphne wine when the fight broke out. Their conversation had been growing more romantic and they were even holding hands. When they heard Gorski's yell, Frazier looked up to see his friends in a fist fight against approximately five to one odds with more *Colorado* crew men and women rushing in the bar to join the fray. He jumped to his feet as did Papanikolaou. She took the empty wine bottle in her left hand, just in case.

The first one in to defend the cadets was Drayton Love-Easter. He grabbed the technician that had hit Rolf with the stool and, with a right cross, hit him in the nose. The technician's nose broke, blood spilling down onto his chin and the front of his uniform. Love-Easter spun around and took the bleeding technicians legs out from under him. The impact stunned the technician. Love-Easter turned his attention to two computer technicians that were charging at him. They both had bottles of ale held above their heads in their hands with the intent to hit Love-Easter with them. They never got the chance. Love-Easter picked up and threw their stunned co-worker at them, sending all three sprawling to the floor.

Six other technicians rushed at Love-Easter, brandishing stools, bottles and one had pulled a knife. Love-Easter quickly ripped a table out of the floor and lifted it over his head. The six charging opponents slowed their advance, impressed by Love-Easter's strength. Recognizing their hesitation, Love-Easter threw the table at the man with the knife and then charged the others and drop kicked one. The other four tried to swing at Love-Easter, but he was too fast for them. He kicked another in the face, and hit a fourth in the stomach with his right fist. It was almost unfair Love-Easter thought to himself, even outnumbered, these men were no match for a well-trained Spetsnaz graduate.

Frazier had rushed into the middle of the fray, delivering a drop kick to Ilyasova with his left leg to the officer's chest, sending him crashing to the floor. Gorski, Staszko, and the Andolini's were in the middle of the brawl, throwing punches and kicks as the odds against them were five to one. Papanikolaou followed them with one fist clenched around the empty wine bottle.

Harcourt kicked with his right leg and connected with one of his opponents and sent him flailing to the floor. Harcourt head butted the man to his left, who released Harcourt's arm. Using his freed left arm, Harcourt punched the man holding his right arm in the mouth. That man released Harcourt as well and fell to his knees. Harcourt showed his three adversaries no mercy. He began kicking them while they were down. He was not about to give any of them another chance to get back on their feet and get the best of him.

Gorski took on Griffin, who seemed to enjoy boxing by the way he held his fists and moved his body as he fought. Gorski jabbed, bobbed and side stepped several of Griffin's punches until he was able to get a few body shots in. Gorski hit Griffin under the jaw with his left fist, stunning the Lieutenant. Gorski finished him off with a right hook across the jaw. Griffin was knocked out cold.

Gorski saw Staszko using her martial arts training with pinpoint accuracy. She was spinning and kicking men in the heads, chests and backsides. In a matter of sixty seconds she had downed five men and three women.

Papanikolaou ducked the reaching arms of the giant that had thrown Fenster on to the bar table. He jumped on a bar stool then leaped up in the air and smashed her empty wine bottle across the man's head. The giant technician fell to the ground without even a whimper.

The Andolini brothers were side by side, punching combatants. At their feet were three unconscious technicians. Dominic and Marco were great fighters and Gorski was glad they were on his side. The *Colorado* crew members foolishly kept rushing the Italians and, one by one, the twin brothers dispatched them with little effort.

That was when the Space Station Security charged into Tinkerbelle's with stun guns blazing. The Andolini brothers were both stunned in the back as were several crew men from the *Colorado.* The fight quickly stopped and everyone put their hands up.

Gorski noticed that the birthday boy, Drew Harrison, was passed out in his chair from all of the tequila and whiskey shots he had been doing. He had missed out on the action.

A Marine Lieutenant entered the bar. He had the insignia patch of Space Station Cy-7 on his shoulder and his name patch read Garrison. He walked around to the scared bar staff and inspected the broken tables. Garrison slowly walked over to Ilyasova, reached down with both hands and grabbed the front of his uniform. Garrison picked him up from the ground and looked him in the eyes. "What the hell happened here?"

Ilyasova looked around and wiped the blood out of his mouth on his uniform sleeve. "These cadets attacked me and my crew members without provocation. They should be arrested and expelled from the Academy."

Garrison looked over to Gorski and his group. "What do you have to say for yourselves?" Gorski looked for Gillis and remembered he had already left upstairs with the girl. Gillis was always their Cicero, he knew how to speak to authority figures and plead their case.

Love-Easter stepped forward, "Sir that man is lying! His men started this fight. He was doing things that warranted us to step in, to protect our lady friend from his advances. Instead of letting the situation be, he and his crew members attacked us. We defended ourselves from deadly force."

Garrison nodded as he took in the information, "Well, you are all under temporary house arrest. I am chief of security on this station and I will personally view the security tapes and determine what action is appropriate." He motioned to the six soldiers that had been standing behind him in silence. "Take them all to the Tank."

The Tank was infamous among military service men and women. It was the one place that one did not want to end up in. It was a slang term for prison or holding cells. Generally, the worst of the worst ended up in the Tank. Once incarcerated in the Tank, the guards generally let the prisoners fend for themselves. Rape, killings, beatings and maiming occurred with regularity in the Tank. And there was no difference regarding the horrible conditions across the Earth Empire. The politicians insisted upon it. It was widely believed by correctional experts that if the Tank was feared, it would act as deterrence to criminal activity.

Gorski and his group and the crew from the *Colorado* were escorted down to the lower level of the space station. They were put in two separate large holding cells. The individuals that had been stunned were starting to wake up, with massive headaches. Klaus had a split lower lip; Fenster had cuts on his back and neck. Rolf was also cut on his arms and back.

Ilyasova looked at the cadets through the bars after the

guards left them. "You will all be forced into the enlisted ranks for this. You assaulted officers of the Space Command! I hope some of you end up on the Colorado so I can personally toss your ass out of the airlock and watch you die."

Mejia, who had been treating Klaus' busted lip stood up and walked over to the metal bars separating the two groups. "You are a pinche puto! When they see the tapes and what you were doing! If I see you again, I will cut your testicles off and force them down your throat and make you choke on them!"

Ilyasova laughed, "Really? You were enjoying the attention. Don't act all offended now, chica. Yes, I know your language. Your careers are over before they even begin. When you get kicked out of the Academy I will make sure you get transferred to my ship and make you my personal sex slave."

Love-Easter walked over and stood next to Mejia and put his arm around her shoulders to hold her back. She was ready to let loose with an emotional tirade against Ilyasova. "So you admit to fondling this lady in public? Exposing her body in public?"

Ilyasova laughed, "Yes, so what? She wanted me to do it."

Love-Easter nodded and motioned over to Klaus, "And you admit that when my friend over there came to rescue the lady, you and your men started a fight with him."

Ilyasova was still laughing and pointed at Klaus. "Hell yes. You punk kids are about to learn the hard way that officers will be believed over you any day of the week. You should learn to mind your own business. If you would have stayed out of it, the whole bar would have gotten a great show."

Mejia had he fists balled up and was scowling at the arrogant flight officer. "What kind of show are you talking about?"

Jahn answered this time, "We were going to all three take turns having sex with you on the table. Everyone was going to watch and enjoy the exhibition. You would have gotten laid by three horny pilots so you would have been happy and everyone here would have been treated to free live porno action."

"If I see the three of you ever again, I will gut you," Mejia walked away and went back to Klaus' side. Mejia was beyond anger and rather than let herself get into a shouting match she elected to sit next to the man that had protected her. The fact that Ilyasova planned to disgrace her in such a manner made her blood boil. She began to appreciate the kind hearted Klaus even more. By coming to her aid, he was her hero.

The prisoners heard several sets of footsteps approaching. Eight uniformed individuals stopped in front of their cells, Lieutenant Garrison was one of them. He stood in front of the cells and motioned for his guards to encircle the jail entrances. A female captain walked through the Marines and was glaring at the men and women from the *Colorado*. Gorski could tell that Ilyasova and the *Colorado* group were taken aback by the captain's presence. Her name tag read Ruiz and her arm patch insignia on her blue one piece uniform was from the U.N.S.C. Colorado. She was their captain. Captain Ruiz was about the same height as Mejia and had dark eyes, dark hair with a few grey strands showing. Ruiz was in her fifties, very fit due to her strict adherence to a round of tennis every day and abdominal exercises that kept her stomach flat and muscular.

Garrison cleared his throat to get the attention of the prisoners. "I looked at the tapes. Does anyone here have anything to say before we take statements?"

Griffin pointed an accusatory finger at Klaus and Mejia, "They started this."

Love-Easter stepped forward and pulled out of his breast pocket a small computer device. He held to Garrison and Captain Ruiz. "Computer, play back the conversation I just had with Lieutenant Commander Ilyasova."

The device played back every word, with clarity. Ruiz and Garrison were glaring at the *Colorado* crew members.

Without addressing her crew first, Ruiz looked over to Mejia to get her position. "Miss, you do wish to press charges on this?

Mejia stood up and approached Ruiz, "Yes, ma'am, I do. The officers' behavior was unbecoming and they were disgracing me in front of everyone. Most importantly, those three men were in uniform when they did it. They disgraced the service, themselves and the U.N.S.C. Colorado."

Ruiz nodded in agreement with Mejia, "You will make a fine officer one day young lady." She turned her attention to the crew members. "Lieutenant Commander Ilyasova, you are hereby administratively demoted to Ensign. Jahn and Griffin, the same demotion applies to you. You are referred to Space Command custody for court martial and are fired from my command. Your pay is suspended. My chief of security will box up your belongings and have them delivered to you. Neither one of you will maintain your security clearance to gain admission aboard the Colorado. The rest of you are suspended for one month without pay and ordered to report back to the Colorado within the hour."

Ruiz looked back over to Mejia and was smiling at her, "It is difficult being a woman in a man's world. Watch your back. I had to fight to obtain my command and I'll be damned before any man or woman I command disgraces our service. My apologies and best wishes to all of you."

Garrison motioned to the guards, "Release the cadets."

The bars slid opened so that Gorski and his entourage could leave the place called the Tank. One by one the cadets walked out.

Mejia ran to catch up with Captain Ruiz. She met the older woman at the escalator.

"Ma'am, I wanted to thank you for what you did back there," Mejia said.

Ruiz stopped walking and faced the young cadet, "You

should be more careful young lady. You could have been hurt physically and emotionally. I have wanted to rid myself of Ilyasova for the last year. You are not the first woman he has been inappropriate with. But you are the first to stand up to him and press charges. Thanks to you, I can begin to search for a new pilot. You are very lucky to have friends that will stand up for you"

Mejia nodded, "I know."

"Let me speak bluntly with you. You remind me of myself when I was your age. I used to dress like you do and I slept with several pilots. I was enamored with men in uniform. But, in time, I learned that they just used me." Ruiz put her hands on Mejia's shoulders. "I watched the tapes of what happened in that bar. I never had friends like yours, to fight for me like they did. Count your blessings and stop dressing like a prostitute. You are like fly paper in those clothes and the only thing you will attract is trouble. You need to find a serious man, one that will be there for you when you need him to be." Ruiz stepped onto the escalator. "By the way, when you graduate, look me up. I have three openings for pilots and that offer stands for your friends as well. I could use a few crew members that are willing to fight for what is right."

CHAPTER FIVE

The bar named O'Malley's was packed, as was normal for a Friday night. O'Malley's was a popular destination for the cadets at Clovis Academy on Clovis City, planet New Edinburgh. Each weekend, students would show up to relieve the pressure of their studies or examinations. They would arrive in groups, dates or come alone. The owner, Paddy O'Malley, had opened the bar ten years earlier and was making a great living on the local university crowd. He had moved his location twice, each time to a much larger location than the one before it. His newest version of O'Malley's was five floors, each floor with its' own bar and a different theme from the others. Paddy O'Malley had installed a large kitchen in his new location, serving finger foods, pizzas, steaks, and foods from the old country such as Shepherd Pie and various soups featuring cabbage and potatoes.

Each floor had a minimum of forty-thousand square feet. The first floor of the new O'Malley's featured a sports theme with pool tables, big screen monitors showing the latest and greatest events from the eight solar systems sports contests. The second floor had a dance theme, no tables and a large dance floor. The third floor was a restaurant. The fourth floor was a computerized gaming room with the most advanced three dimensional war games. The fifth floor was a location for students to sit and meet, study, sing on stage, play chess and meet.

The fifth floor was generally frequented by the more serious students. Other than the live music on Saturday nights, there was less noise so they could have conversations without shouting over loud music. Each table on the fifth floor was equipped with microchips for universal compute access. With that technology, the customer at each table could watch the current events, access any website and chat with family and friends across the galaxies.

O'Malley had hired mainly female cadets as his employees; their uniforms were skin tight outfits in the colors of orange tube tops, green miniskirts and white boots. The workers were either greeters at the front door, bartenders or waitresses. The kitchen staff was hidden behind the walls and was mostly family members of the owner, and never made contact with the customers.

Cadet senior Siobhan Collins walked into the front

entrance of O'Malley's and was greeted by a hostess. Collins told the employee that she was meeting friends on the fifth floor. Collins ran to the stairs, oblivious to the off-duty soldiers and private industry pilots that stared at her with lust in their eyes. Her long, flowing red hair and athletic figure seemed to always attract the attention of men. She was almost six feet tall and was full of confidence. She kept her head up, ignoring the whistles and rude comments from the miners and pilots at the bars that were given for the purpose of catching her attention. She had changed out of her medical training uniform from the Academy into a pair of black shorts, white blouse and tennis shoes. She had a pair of jade earrings on that matched her gold necklace with a jade stud dangling from it. Collins skipped every other step on the winding stair case all the way up to the fifth floor where her older sister, Ginger Collins O'Grady, was waiting.

Siobhan Collins looked around the large room and noted that there was a full crowd and all of the tables were taken. The bar was full of military personnel, private pilots, business men and women, rogues, a few Kotek's, instructors from the Academy, prostitutes and cadets. Collins found her sister sitting in a half moon booth around a large table. Ginger Collins O'Grady looked similar to her sister Siobhan as far as physical appearance. However, due to Ginger's chosen career, she was always dressed in a business suit. Ginger worked for her father at the United Nations Administration Building as a computer information analyst and was a master of programming computers and analyzing data. She also had won several competitions on the computer gaming circuit. She loved three dimensional war games and excelled at the craft. Most of the pre-teen and teenage children were not ready for the competition when Ginger would challenge them. She had her hair cut short and was never out in public without dressing professionally due to the rules requiring her to maintain the image that the employees of the United Nations were the best and the brightest. It was drilled into the minds of all United Nations employees that they were all Ambassadors of the Glorious Leader and therefore must maintain a professional image to the people. That was the mandate of the Glorious Leader, Vladimir Sikorsky, and any violation of that rule would result in termination of employment. Ginger had been married for one year, to a cadet named Eamon O'Grady, who was studying for his doctorate at the Academy.

Ginger was relaxing in a booth with two other girls from the Academy. Siobhan ran over to her sister and they immediately hugged each other. Siobhan sat down next to her and noticed the other two cadets. Siobhan had met one of the women several times before. Her name was Sophia DuBravac, a very alluring cadet junior from France or Belgium, Siobhan could not recall from which nation. DuBravac was close friends to Julia Steiner, another cadet that was dating the younger brother of Siobhan and Ginger. Steiner had introduced DuBravac to the Collins family and they had accepted her without question. Ginger's husband was suspicious of both Steiner and DuBravac, as they had once been members of the infamous Gorski Gang. DuBravac later became more closely involved with the Collins family when she started dating Les Gillis, who had been a good friend to each of Siobhan's siblings and would spend some of his spare time with the family.

The Gorski Gang and the Collins family had been cool toward each other over the years. Part of the reason was that Siobhan had been Yuri Gorski's first girlfriend. The relationship between Siobhan and Gorski did not end badly, it just faded away. They were still friends and cordial to each other. Siobhan's family, however, had hard feelings toward Gorski and given Gorski's actions as a carouser and reputation as a trouble maker, it all added up to an unspoken edict that Yuri Gorski was not welcome around Collins family functions. Eamon O'Grady had the strongest feelings against Gorski and his Gang. O'Grady believed that the Gorski faction was disrespectful to the corps, insubordinate, caustic and not worthy to be officers in the Space Command. The only member of Gorski's group that accepted by the Collins' family was Les Gillis. The Collins clan respected and admired those that excelled academically and Gillis was a straight "A" student. Gillis was also a fellow Irishman. The Collins family had come to New Edinburgh from Boston, Massachusetts Territory while Gillis was from Ireland. They would come together occasionally and sing songs together, old songs from the Emerald Isle and Boston. It was a fellowship that Gillis and the Collins family deeply enjoyed.

Siobhan recognized the other woman present as cadet sophomore Lila Zapata. Siobhan knew the Zapata girl well as they were on the Academy chess team. Zapata was still shy and unsure of herself even though she had a body for sin and a remarkably beautiful face. Men would make advances at Zapata, but she was awkward in the ways of romance and therefore not receptive. Siobhan wondered if Zapata liked men at all or whether she understood the basic instinct to procreate. Zapata seemed shocked at times by things that happened around her and was gullible and inexperienced in the ways of the world. She also seemed to lack common sense. But, if you needed a nuclear engine repaired in record timing, she could perform that task with her eyes closed. She was brilliant in her knowledge of engineering and weaponry. She was almost always reading some new research paper or thesis and wanting to talk about the conclusions. Most men would tune her out because she was far more intelligent than the majority of them. DuBravac seemed to be very protective of Zapata, always watching out for her.

The women had drinks on the table, Zapata drinking an orange-cranberry juice blend that was in a red crystal tall glass, DuBravac had a stein of beer and Ginger O'Grady had a martini glass sitting in front of her. There was a plate on the center of the table with fried Jumper tail bites and red sauce. The Jumper was a large meat eating reptile that was indigenous to the planet New Edinburgh. The Jumpers were fast, smart and would kill and eat a human in no time. The meat of a Jumper was delicious, almost the flavor and texture of chicken. The chef had a beer batter recipe for the fried Jumper tail bites that was famous throughout the population of Clovis City. The bar also had its' own brewery that was located in another province of New Edinburgh. The beer, ale, and some of the bestselling whiskey brands were owned by the O'Malley family.

Siobhan hugged DuBravac and Zapata.

"Well, our mutual friend did it again," Siobhan announced to the group.

"Did what? Who?" Zapata was wide eyed. She was holding her glass of juice tightly in her left fist as if she thought something bad was coming.

"Calm down, Lila," Siobhan told her. "Yuri and his gang got into a bar fight on Cy-7. News reports say that the entire group was arrested and taken to the Tank."

DuBravac looked startled by the news. Her heart sank as she thought of her ex-boyfriend getting into trouble. Although DuBravac had ended her relationship with Gillis just before the semester began, she still loved him. "And Les?"

"You know he was there," Ginger said with disdain in her voice. "If Gillis isn't with us, then he is with Gorski. You know that, Sophia."

DuBravac looked over her left shoulder and saw cadet senior Reynita Calderon and her brothers and sisters at another table with cadets James Cobb, Roy Starr, William and Bret Bragg. The Bragg brothers were the leaders of the rival Gang to

Gorski's Gang. There had been many confrontations between the two factions at the Academy over the years. DuBravac noticed that Lupita and Estrellita Calderon had sat down at the Bragg table, each carrying a pitcher of ale to share. DuBravac wondered why the Calderon family members were so loyal to the Bragg's. The Calderon's were known to be good people, while the Bragg's and some of their other followers were the biggest trouble makers on campus.

DuBravac tried to ignore the screams and taunts coming from the Braggs regarding the arrest of the Gorski Gang on Space Station Cy-7. The table had about thirty cadets doing shots of liquor and tequila to celebrate the incarceration of their rivals. Cadet pilot Roy Starr began whistling at DuBravac and calling her to come over to their table.

"Sophia! I love you!" Starr was yelling at her direction.

"Come on, Sophia!" Bret Bragg was laughing. "Come on over here to some real men. Gillis wasn't man enough to keep you satisfied. Come over here and we will give you more loving than you ever thought possible!"

"Ignore them," Siobhan said to DuBravac. "After Yuri and I broke up, several of the Bragg guys tried to bed me. After a while, they gave up trying."

"Bed you? What does that mean?" Zapata blurted out.

"It means that they wanted me to have sex with them," Siobhan answered politely.

DuBravac noticed out of the corner of her eye that cadet

Roy Starr walking toward them. Starr was a devout member of the Bragg faction at the Academy. The Bragg's and Gorski's had many run ins over the years and some of the fist fights had been brutal. DuBravac had participated in more than one of them. Roy Starr had always tried to convince DuBravac to go to his bed, even when she was involved with Gillis. Starr had a dark complexion and was about five feet tall. DuBravac was never interested in the shorter man and she was blunt to him each time he made advances toward her. The fact that Starr persisted in his pursuit of DuBravac proved either Starr was too dense to understand the word no or he loved rejection.

"Sophia!" Starr slurred, clearly inebriated. The four women could smell the ale on his breath. His hair was uncombed and his uniform wrinkled. He leaned over DuBravac and hugged her. He ran his hands all over her back and kissed her neck.

DuBravac pushed his hands off of her. "Roy, you are drunk. Go home."

"Your boyfriend is in jail!" Starr said almost joyful. To Starr, any bad occurrence for Gillis was cause for celebration.

"Back off Roy," Siobhan warned as William Bragg, Bret Bragg and some of the other Bragg gang cheering Starr on. "We are not in the mood for your shit. Go back to your friends."

"But I want to spend some time with lovely Sophia," Starr reached out and ran his fingers through DuBravac's hair.

DuBravac, in a lightning fast move, reached out with her right hand and grabbed Starr's wrist, twisting it. He cried out in pain. She released his wrist and Starr cradled it with his other hand. DuBravac, using her left hand, grabbed Starr by the back of his head and slammed his face onto the table. Starr slumped down to the floor. DuBravac took a drink from her beer, which spilled only a few drops from Starr's head hitting the table.

Starr sat up on his knees and was holding his head.

"Don't ever touch me again," DuBravac warned him. "I will totally annihilate you."

Starr nodded as he slowly stood up and walked back to his friends, who were all laughing at his expense.

"Poor kid. His friends don't care about him," Ginger observed.

"Wow!" Zapata said to DuBravac. "That was really righteous!"

"Righteous?" DuBravac looked at the younger girl. "Where do you get these terms?"

"All the kids are saying it," Zapata told her. "You owned him!"

"Owned him?" Siobhan raised her eyebrows at that one.

"Let's see what happened on Cy-7 shall we?" Ginger suggested. "Computer, display three dimensional news report, regarding recent bar fight on space station Cy-7 involving several cadets from Clovis Academy."

The computer did not verbally respond, but it followed the order. Before the four women appeared a perfect three dimensional scene of the events at Tinkerbelle's bar. The graphics covered the entire table top. They watched as Gorski's Gang fought against six to one odds. The three dimensional broadcast that hovered just inches above their table and extended several feet upwards and left to right was so clear in its' quality, it was as if the four women were actually there, witnessing the event live.

"That was on fire!" Zapata said when the image died down. She turned her attention to DuBravac. "You used to fight like that?"

DuBravac took a sip of her beer, set it down and smiled. "All the time, Lila. I used to "own" everyone." Siobhan chuckled at the use of Zapata's slang term.

"You are so awesome!" Zapata told her.

"I didn't see Les there," Ginger observed.

"If the other side was smart, they would have gone after Les and Drew first. And I did not see Drew either." DuBravac told them. "They are all great fighters, but Drew has the muscle and Les has the brains. If I ever tangled with the Gorski gang, those two would be my first targets."

"But Les was your boyfriend," Siobhan said slowly.

"Precisely," DuBravac nodded. "I feel sorry for anyone that has to fight Les Gillis one on one. Les would," she smiled at Zapata, "he would own them."

"You still love him?" Zapata suddenly blurted out.

DuBravac slowly sipped her beer. DuBravac did not mind the question. She had told Zapata in the past to think first before she blurted out something. DuBravac watched as the waitress delivered a beer to Siobhan. DuBravac waited for the waitress to leave before she responded. "Lila, yes. Yes I do love him. I always will."

"Then why are you sitting here with us?" Zapata asked innocently.

"Because I am stubborn," DuBravac said as she looked down at her beer. "I am full of pride and I don't know how to tell him I was wrong."

The women were silent for a few moments.

Siobhan reached out and held DuBravac's hand. "You need to go back to him. I never saw two people happier together than when it was the two of you."

DuBravac was about to respond when Ginger stood up, almost leaping, with a big smile on her face. "Baby! You made it!"

The other three women watched as their companion ran to her husband, Eamon O'Grady. Husband and wife kissed passionately. The O'Grady's then sat down with the others, Eamon hugging his sister-in-law, Siobhan, and began shaking the hands of Zapata and DuBravac. Zapata thought that Eamon O'Grady was the tallest man she had ever seen and she was impressed with his bulging muscles underneath his skin tight red jogging sweats.

"Wow!" Zapata said to him. She had never met him before. "You are like so hot. Do you go to the gym a lot? Do you have any brothers or cousins for me?"

Eamon O'Grady laughed as he put his arm around Ginger. "All my family is back on old Earth, in Boston. But I will put in a good word for you."

CHAPTER SIX

Caine Rosenburg, Darryl Rosenburg and Avery "Big Bad" Jackson entered the lobby of the Baroness Hotel. They were met by Burton Stapler, another cadet at Achilles Academy. Stapler was a twenty one year old, tall, muscular man, with dark hair and blue eyes. He had several tattoos on his arms, back and legs of death skulls, death holding a scythe and one on his chest of angels being impaled by demons with tridents. He had the satanic symbol tattooed on his left shoulder. He was a rogue, like Jackson, with a checkered past. Stapler would travel with Caine, Alexander and others to New Edinburgh to spend their vacation time at the Rosenburg Ranch. Caine's family had several slave girls that he and his friends could use for their pleasure. Stapler was completely loyal to the Rosenburg family as they allowed him to commit all forms of deviant acts with the slave population.   Stapler also was well aware that slavery was illegal in the eight solar systems, but he would never reveal what he knew of the Rosenburg family. During many summer vacations, Stapler would travel with a member of the Rosenburg hierarchy to force families to give away their children because they could not pay their debts to the Rosenburg Corporation. They would kidnap whole sibling groups, animals, anything of value for the monetary debt. Sometimes they would take the entire family. It was a perfect scheme and no one suspected that the Rosenburg family had such an insidious human trafficking operation behind the scenes of all of their legitimate business endeavors. Stapler was paid well for his assistance to the Rosenburg family slave effort and was occasionally allowed to sexually assault the hostages.

One of the Rosenburg Corporation's legitimate business chains was the Baroness Hotel investment. About twelve years earlier, the matriarch of the Rosenburg family bought the entire eighty-seven location chain of the Baroness Hotels for seventeen billion Empire Dollars. The Rosenburg's controlled and operated the entire business structure.

The manager of the Baroness Hotel on Space Station Cy-7 was a member of the powerful family. Penelope Rosenburg was in her late twenties, blonde and extremely beautiful. She was not a natural beauty, however. Penelope Rosenburg had taken advantage of all of the current, state of the art medical offerings to sculpt her body and revamp her face to recreate her from an average looking lady to a woman that was irresistible. Penelope had perfect teeth due to several medical procedures, perfect hour glass body from implants, waist reduction and bone restructuring. She went from a height of five feet two inches tall to six foot tall by having titanium and other heavy metal grafting to her bones. Muscles from kidnaped women that were harvested by the Rosenburg family for body parts were used to give Penelope fantastic leg tone and shape. It took Penelope several months of physical therapy to learn to walk naturally with the metal extensions to her bone structure. The work was a smashing success, as Penelope moved with grace and the fluidity of a pageant queen. Penelope was also quite intelligent, having attended the best business school on Sikorsky's Planet. She was fluent in a dozen languages, held a bachelor's degree in business administration, a master's in public administration and doctorate in computerized banking.

Stapler, Jackson, Darryl and Caine walked behind the check in station of the Baroness and proceeded down the restricted security corridor after Caine was cleared for access by a palm print scan. The three men entered the executive offices and the few employees present looked up, immediately recognized Caine and ignored his friends. There were several desks made from some of the finest woods and metals in the solar system. Jackson marveled over the three dimensional views of the lobby, the receiving entrance where supplies were delivered, the washrooms, the elevators, and each of the hallways of the six floor hotel. By law, the hotel could not monitor the individual rooms but were required to monitor the hallways.

Caine led them to another hallway and to a door that had his sister's assumed name etched into the sliding glass front. All of the Rosenburg family members that were placed in positions of authority to manage family assets would take on an alias. The purpose was for the ability to deflect and thwart any investigations into alleged wrongdoing. Criminal Investigation Division detectives and military security officers were generally too dense to connect the dots on many crimes. The assumed names were extra protection to the family, to ensure no liability would ever attach.

Caine and his men entered Penelope's office. Another palm scan was required to go further, which Caine passed, and the three men entered the Management office. Penelope was there, waiting for them in her dark leather swivel chair behind her dark desk carved from lava rock. She was wearing a purple sweater, black long skirt and heeled shoes. Her hair was long and straight.

"About time, little brother. What took you so long?" Penelope Rosenburg said as a greeting. She was a very busy woman and had little time or patience for Caine's little games. Caine, like several of Penelope's siblings, was a homicidal maniac. Penelope had told her father on more than one occasion, to send Caine away for psychiatric help. She believed him to be a serial killer that should be in jail. Her father denied each of her requests.

"We were held up. Seems there was a fight at one of the

bars and security was making sure all of the offenders were located." Caine said while he sat down in one of the visitor's chairs. "You remember my friends?"

"Yes, please have a seat," Penelope motioned. This was not the first time Caine and his demented friends had come to the Hotel demanding access to some woman. Penelope was afraid to ask her next set of questions. "What devious acts are you up to that require me to divert my attention away from running this establishment? And now you have Darryl getting involved in your twisted acts?"

Caine pulled out two color photographs and handed them to his sister. He ignored her criticism of their hunt. In Caine's mind, Penelope was an intellectual nerd and would never understand the thrill of killing. "We believe these two girls are guests here. We want them."

Penelope looked at the two photos, "Very pretty." She walked over to a computer desk, set the photographs down, side by side. "Computer, scan these photos and see if we have any matches on our current guest log."

The computer quickly answered, "Elektra Papanikolaou is on the fifth floor in room 544. April Mejia is on the third floor in room 333."

Caine Rosenburg was smiling, clapping his hands together. "I knew it."

Penelope shook her finger at her younger half-sibling, "I run a legitimate business here. You better not do anything that will disturb my guests or harm the reputation of this profitable establishment. Your appetite for women is going to get our family into trouble one day. I have told father several times to speak with you about this."

Caine leaned forward and snarled at her, "Yes, but my mother is the current favorite of father. So, I will be the one that gets what he wants. And, what I want, what we want, is complete access to levels three and five and complete access to rooms 544 and 333. I want all security cameras turned off for the next three hours so there is no evidence of our having been here. Think you can handle that simple request, sister?"

"Caine," Penelope said with agitation in her voice. "Why these two girls? There is a universe filled with attractive women. The Ranch has thousands of slave girls that will do whatever you want. These two? Why?"

Caine shrugged, "Because they are a challenge. Because we like them and we want them. Mostly, we want to hear them scream when we slice them up after we have finished with them."

Penelope looked over the men; her wrinkled nose indicated her disgust with them. But, she knew Caine had the upper hand. Father always catered to Caine's mother. "Okay, say I let you rape these girls, torture and kill them. Is there any chance this will come back on us? I mean, are these girls connected in any way politically? Are they from the Allen family? The Fenster's? The Brackenridge family? What kind of exposure would our family be getting into if you cannot cover this up?"

Caine stood up and began pacing, "They are both from Clovis Academy and from Earth originally. They have no family here. They have a few friends in the hotel, but they are all cadets as well. I have some other friends that will be helping. We will get the first girl, have our fun with her and then take her down the security corridor to be disposed of. Then we'll get the second girl. No big deal. Their classmates will assume they left earlier than they planned and no one will be the wiser. We can program the shuttle computers to record that the two girls left the Space Station tonight."

"You have it all planned out," Penelope said under her breath. "Tell me, Caine, if I were not your half-sister, would you and your friends want to rape and butcher me, too?"

"I would!" Stapler said quickly, admiring Penelope's face and body. "Hell yeah. With your body? You would be fun."

Penelope crossed her arms under her large breasts disapprovingly. At least Stapler was honest. A psychopath, but honest. "All right. I will inform the hotel security chief to shut down all surveillance for the next three hours. Obviously I recommend that the four of you seek out some psychiatric assistance, but I am certain you are all unwilling to do so. Caine, why? Why do you do this?"

Caine smiled at his sibling and laughed. "Because it is fun. The look in their eyes, just as you gut them open, the hopelessness in their voices as they are begging for their lives. It is the greatest rush I have ever experienced. Why? Why would I do this? Because I can. And why are you so against it? All your cosmetic surgery required body parts from other young girls. How many young women did you kill to get the right skin color, the muscle tone for your legs and gluteus maximus? How about your full breasts? Your cheek bones? Your teeth? Who did the family harvest those from? Do you even know their names? Did you ever call their families and express any condolences for the untimely deaths of their loved ones? "

"Get the hell out of here," Penelope snarled. She knew Caine was correct about her. She did not know how many had been sacrificed by her father during the time she had her body and face worked on by the family surgeons. She estimated about a dozen nameless girls gave their lives for all of her physical changes. Sometimes in her sleep, Penelope would dream of women accusing her of murder. She would wake up in a cold sweat, regretting that she had allowed her father to force her to participate in such obscene acts. "Do what you need to."

Caine waived his left hand at his two men and Darryl. "Let's go. Get the others, three hours will go fast."

As the men left her office, Penelope started the cover up. "Computer, burn the two photographs on the computer scan." She watched as a red laser shot from the top of the picture scanner and the photos of the two girls destined to die began to burn. "Delete any evidence of the meeting in my office. Give

Caine and Darryl Rosenburg full access to floors three and five. Also, record that the tenant in Room 333 checked out at this very moment. Record that the tenant in Room 544 checked out with her."

CHAPTER SEVEN

After their release from the Tank, the members of Gorski's Gang had retired to their individual rooms at the Hotel. They had decided to meet the next day at eleven for brunch and continue with their weekend of fun and relaxation.

Archibald Frazier walked Elektra Papanikolaou to her room on the fifth floor. Frazier was hopeful that the time he spent with her at Tinkerbelle's was the beginning of something special between them. She was smart and did not ridicule him for studying geology as other women at the Academy had done to him in the past. He was unsure whether or not she felt the same for him. When they arrived at her door, Frazier awkwardly kissed her on the cheek. She smiled, embraced him and kissed him full on the lips. They kissed for several minutes until she pulled away.

"What's wrong?" Frazier wanted to know.

Papanikolaou sighed and took his hands in hers, "I really like you. Too much, probably. I would love to invite you in and have you stay the night. But, um, I think that we should spend more time getting to know each other first."

Frazier nodded that he had no objection to her feelings on the issue. He wanted to make love to the woman more than anything, but he was willing to wait as long as it took. He had never thought he would get as close to her as he was at that moment. "I understand. Let's, take things slow. I really like you too."

She kissed him again, said good night and disappeared into her room.

Frazier began walking when the door across the hall from Papanikolaou opened. Frazier saw Love-Easter standing there, wearing blue work out sweats and smoking a cigarette.

"She's an amazing lady," Love-Easter said to him.

"Yes she is," Frazier agreed.

Love-Easter passed the cigarette to the younger man. "Here, take a hit. It's good stuff."

"What is it?"

"Marijuana from the virgin forest region. It is legal."

Frazier took a long puff off of the cigarette and began coughing. "Strong stuff," he said with a raspy voice.

Love-Easter laughed. "Yes, but good." Frazier passed him the cigarette back and Love-Easter smoked some more. "Yuri and Jen are coming up in a bit. Why don't you hang with us? I have a big stash here."

Frazier shrugged, his hands were still sore from the bar fight and he had some bruises from a few punches he took from some of their opponents. "I am kind of tired."

Love-Easter sensed that the young lad was depressed that Papanikolaou did not invite him in. "Look, I understand you want the girl. You have to be patient." He passed the cigarette to Frazier who took another hit from it. He passed it back to Love-Easter. "She is a good girl. Like the rest of us, she is here on this new planet at the Academy trying to find her way in life. She is alone with no family here, just as we were when we left Earth to come to study here. She has been sweet to all of us. She cooks for us, she is warm and caring. This is not a woman you pick up at a bar. This is a woman you love forever and have your children with."

Frazier looked back at her door, "I agree. I do care about her. A lot."

"Good. Because one day, she will ask you to come inside her room. And, she will let you take her to bed." Love-Easter smoked from the marijuana cigarette. "Just make sure when that day comes, you take her to bed because you want her forever. I am telling you from experience. You have a chance that most men screw up badly. A quality lady is hard to find in this life. Don't be one of the men that blow it."

Frazier smoked some more, beginning to feel light headed. "And you? Did you ever have a girl, like Elektra, one that was special?"

Love-Easter nodded, his eyes looking around the hallway. "Yes, yes I did. A few years ago. I blew it. I was young and stupid and I lost her. I begged for another chance, even though I knew I did not deserve it. She rightfully refused me. I know I hurt her. She married another man recently and he is very fortunate to have her in his life."

"Maybe another one will come along," Frazier said hopefully, taking another smoke off the marijuana cigarette.

"Not like her," Love-Easter said with regret, remembering the lost love of his life. "Don't be an idiot like me. Give that girl all your love and attention and loyalty. You will be a better man for it."

Frazier nodded, "Thanks for the advice. I feel kind of dizzy."

"Great stuff, isn't it? Hold on." Love-Easter stepped back in his room for a few seconds. He reappeared with four marijuana cigarettes. "Here, take these and share them with Dirk, Klaus and the others. Enjoy."

Frazier took them, "Thanks."

"Have a good night!"

Frazier walked away, thinking long and hard about Love-Easter's advice.

In Room 333 April Mejia stepped out of the shower and began drying off with one of the Hotel towels. She was still shaken up by the events of the evening. She did not want to be alone; terrified that another unwanted advance on her was imminent. She asked the room automated computer to turn on the hair dryer. Warm air hit her wet head from six different directions. After a few minutes, she knew her hair was dry and asked the computer to stop. She stepped into her bed room and began to dress. She asked computer to raise Harumi Shigeta's room. And there was no response. Most likely she was with her on-again off-again boyfriend Dominic Andolini.

Mejia found a white bathrobe with the gold Hotel insignia etched into the left top. She put on a pair of slippers and made a decision that probably saved her life. She left her room and walked several doors down on the plush mauve carpeting and knocked.

Klaus Rhinehard heard the knock at his door, "Computer, open door."

The door opened and Mejia walked in. Klaus saw her wearing the white bathrobe and thought that she looked beautiful. He was practically speechless to see her standing in his doorway.

"I wanted some company," Mejia told him, sensing that he was unable to think of something to say. "I hope it is okay if I stay a while. I just wanted someone to talk to and since you are my knight in shining armor, I picked you."

Klaus motioned for her to come in. "Yes, please. I would love the company." He was surprised that she would choose to come to him, but he was elated that she did. He didn't think that taking a few punches for Mejia would make such an impression with her.

Mejia walked in and the door slid shut behind her.

Harumi Shigeta also did not wish to be alone and her night had been pre-arranged before she left planet New Edinburgh. After being released from the Tank, Shigeta cleaned up, showered, changed clothes and then made her way to Dominic Andolini's room. He had been expecting her and welcomed her in. They began kissing passionately as the doors slide shut behind her. They both could not undress each other fast enough. They had been involved off and on for two years, keeping their relationship secret. Their cultural upbringing had been very different, but that had been part of the initial attraction. After their many passionate moments together, they would lie next to each other teaching one another about their homes on Earth. Dominic would have Shigeta teach him Japanese words and phrases. Shigeta was also fascinated with learning Italian from him. Their comfort level with one another had grown strong over time.

After they made love and were cuddled in each other's arms Shigeta told Dominic that she was in love with him. He kissed her on the lips gently and ran his hands through her hair. He told her that he loved her as well. It was not the first time the couple had expressed their mutual feelings for one another, nor would it be the last. They spent the rest of the evening discussing their future life together.

Marco Andolini had showered, dressed and made his way to the lobby of the hotel. He walked out into the main concourse of the space station and continued on to the bar called the Straight Flush. Marco was a huge fan of Texas Hold 'Em and he knew that the Straight Flush had nightly cash games. In addition, the Straight Flush had a reputation for attracting the most attractive women on the entire space station. Marco's brother Dominic did not like card playing, so that left Marco on his own whenever there was a casino nearby.

Michel Darcel Evart had finished his time with the man he met at Tinkerbelle's. His name was Brad, an international trade lawyer that had been traveling through en route to Sikorsky's Planet. Brad proved to be a great lover.   Evart was a very fit man, with broad shoulders and muscular abdomen. His legs were lean due to his running several kilometers every other day. He had dark hair and light blue eyes. Evart spent much of his spare time in the gymnasium with his friends Harrison, Love-Easter, Gillis and Gorski. Evart was twenty-one years old, six foot two inches tall with perfect teeth and a kind smile. He sported a razor thin mustache as a tribute to his love of the old swashbuckler movies of old Hollywood.

Evart asked the computer to call Yuri Gorski's room.

"This is Jen,"

Evart smiled at the sound of her voice. He had always liked Staszko. She was a classic beauty. Hundreds of years ago, she would have been a big screen starlet, making movies with Errol Flynn and other actors that Evart loved to watch. She had poise, fantastic legs and a level of unpredictability that would keep any man by her side. Evart would always kid her, that if he had been heterosexual, he would have fought Gorski for her affections."

"This is Michel," Evart announced. "How are you all doing?"

Staszko laughed, "Not as well as you, according to Les."

Evart laughed as well, "Yes, he was so gorgeous. I could not resist his advances. What are the plans for the rest of the night?"

"Well, Yuri is showering and we were going to meet Les up in Dray's room. Dray scored some prime grade MJ so we thought we would all get high."

Evart laughed as he dressed, "Sounds like a great way to end a marvelous evening. Count me in."

"Well, come up to our room. Les is on his way and we can all go up together," Staszko told him.

"See you in a few seconds," Evart then told the computer to end the conversation.

Les Gillis stepped out of his shower and saw Alejandra Khartov, stretching out on his bed. Gillis allowed her to sleep longer when he had snuck off to the shower.

"Hey, you're awake," Gillis said playfully.

Khartov sat up quickly, her eyes showed the look of

panic. "What time is it?"

Gillis shrugged, "A little after eleven p.m. We are going upstairs to meet some of my..."

He was cut off short as Khartov swore, tossed the covers from the bed. "I have to go!"

"What? Why?" Gillis hoped for an explanation.

Khartov started grabbing her clothes that were scattered all around the hotel room. "My damn husband will be arriving soon! I have to get back to the docking bay to meet him!"

"Husband?" Gillis asked, plopping down in a chair.

Khartov ran to Gillis and kissed him on the cheek. "I know I should have told you, but I was concerned you wouldn't have sex with me if I did. You go to your friends. I am going to use your shower and I'll let myself out." She kissed Gillis on the cheek again. "You are a great lover."

Gillis laughed as she carried her clothing into the bathroom, "Glad you think so."

She was in the shower quickly. Gillis threw on a pair of pants and shirt and left the Hotel Room. He walked rapidly down the third floor hallway toward the elevator. He knew that his friends would kid him over the incident since he was always thought of as having terrible luck with the ladies. Married? Damn, at least there were no worries of a commitment with Khartov. As he walked, he scratched the back of his head. He never saw that one coming his way. She seemed single. Khartov's friends at Tinkerbelle's never said anything suspicious.

Gillis decided that he should let the situation go and chalk it up to experience.

Gillis arrived at Gorski's room and Staszko greeted him as Gorski was in the shower. Staszko asked where Gillis' new woman was and he responded by telling her that the woman was married. Staszko laughed and hugged him playfully.

"Ah, Les. Reynita, Sophia, Melissa, Maria, and now Alejandra! How come this always happens to you?" Staszko asked him as he walked quickly over to the bottles of liquor that were on the window mantle on the far side of the room.

Gillis found a glass and poured himself a shot of whiskey, "You forgot about Trina, Candi and Karina. They all burned me, too."

"No, not Candi." Staszko recalled the story that Gorski had told her about the girl. "Pour me a shot while you are there. Candi was a senior when you were just starting your stay at Clovis City and she graduated and moved on to her assignment. She did not burn you. Yuri said she was up front about her career plans. So Candi cannot be ridiculed. Nor can Sophia, she was always honest."

Gillis handed her a glass of whiskey. He downed a second shot and thought for a moment, "Sophia was the best."

Soon after Gillis sat down in the chairs and continued to drink and reminisce about Gillis' past lovers, Evart arrived with a bottle of wine from his family estate in France. Gorski finished in the shower and joined Evart, Gillis and Staszko to drink wine and catch up on the day's events.

Caine Rosenburg, Darryl Rosenburg, Avery Jackson, Burton Stapler and three others, Kai Chin, Peter Lomax and Cleon Alexander walked rapidly into the lobby of the Baroness Hotel. They moved directly to the hotel elevator with purpose. There was no hesitation with the men as they were on a mission to hunt and murder two beautiful women. Caine told them their first destination was the third floor. As they walked, they kept their faces forward while their eyes roamed from side to side, searching for any police or soldiers that might interrupt their plans.

Kai Chin was the shortest man in the group. He was a student at the Achilles Academy and had recognized that being a close friend with a Rosenburg was an astute career move. Caine included Chin on the hunts due to his talents with martial arts and weaponry. Chin was not as sadistic as the others and did not take part in the rape or torture of the victims. Chin was there for the pay and Caine compensated him handsomely to watch their backs during the capture, rape and torture of the victims. Chin also knew how to remain silent regarding things he had seen. He secretly hoped that his association with the Royal Family connected Rosenburg clan would earn him a position in the prestigious Military Intelligence of the Space Command.

Peter Lomax was also a cadet at the Achilles Academy. He was studying astral navigation and was training to hone his piloting skills. Lomax would generally jump in on the attack if he thought the female victim was sexy enough for his needs. His main duty was to fly the getaway private ship, with the chopped up bodies of the victims. Lomax enjoyed how well Caine paid for his assistance. At his school, Lomax was the star point guard of the Academy Basketball team. He often would brag about his triple double average from the previous season of competition.

Cleon Alexander was a cadet senior at the Achilles Academy. He was every bit a serial killer as Jackson, Stapler and Caine. Alexander had been friends with Jackson and it was Jackson that had introduced Caine to him. He was loyal because, with Caine by his side he could meet his sadistic needs. Alexander cared little for the Empire dollars he was paid by Caine but accepted the money nonetheless. He enjoyed inflicting pain on others and had become adept with a knife and skinning pretty young women alive. He had recently taken several gardening tools and converted them into weapons of torture.

The seven men walked quickly up the stairs and find themselves on the third floor. The hallway was empty, which was great news for the would-be rapists. No witnesses. They moved with a purpose to room 333 and Caine verbally ordered the computer to open the door. They watched as the door slid open. Jackson and Alexander were the first two in, followed by Stapler and Caine. Their goal was to catch the victim by surprise and keep her from screaming for help. That was always the hardest part. If they screamed, and others heard, then they would have to abort. But on this raid they found the room empty. April

Mejia was nowhere to be found. All of the men, save Chin, were in the room. Stapler searched the bathroom and pulled open the shower curtain to see if she were hiding there.

"Where is she?" Lomax asked.

Caine smashed his fist on a table, "Damn! I was certain she would be here."

They heard a knock on the door and Chin stuck his head inside the room.

"Everything okay?" Chin asked.

Jackson shook his head, "The target is not here."

Chin heard a door further down the hall open and close. He nodded his head in the direction of the sound and Jackson stopped speaking to listen. They heard footsteps approaching them. Chin and Jackson saw Alejandra Khartov walking toward them quickly. The two men did not know that she was on her way to meet her husband at the docking area. Khartov was in a panic as she knew her jealous husband would arrive soon. She would rendezvous with her husband, like the loyal wife, and he would never be the wiser. Khartov had married him for the money. Her husband was overweight and substantially older than she was. But he owned a lucrative business. Khartov laughed to herself when she remembered her marriage vows. Since the wedding ceremony she had been sexually active with forty other men that were not her husband. Men desired her and she wanted to experience being with all of them. She was wearing her business attire that she had on when she first met

Gillis and had inspected the clothing to make sure there was no evidence of her one night stand with the young cadet.

Jackson looked Khartov over and smiled. He nodded to Chin.

Without saying a word, Chin and Jackson approached Khartov. She looked up at the two men, surprised to see them. Her first thought was that they might be some of her husband's employees, sent to spy on her. But she did not recognize either of the men and she knew all of his most loyal workers. Before she could say anything, Chin had his hands over her mouth so she could not scream for help. Khartov's survival instincts kicked in at that moment, realizing that these men represented some form of threat to her well-being. She screamed into Chin's hand as Jackson grabbed her kicking legs and dragged her into Room 333. When they had her in the room the other men realized that their two friends had found a replacement for Mejia. Stapler acted quickly and jammed a two inch long plastic device into Khartov's neck. Chin released Khartov's mouth once Stapler had completed the task.

Khartov tried to scream, but no sound came from her throat. The device that Stapler had planted in her neck was a voice nullifier. Khartov saw that her captors were putting tiny radio receivers into their ears. The receivers were set to the frequency of the voice nullifier in her throat so they could hear her screams while no one else could. The nullifier was another of the long line of creations of the Rosenburg scientists and engineers.

The men began ripping off her clothing. She tried to fight, but they easily overpowered her. Jackson punched Khartov in the face, sending her reeling to the floor. After the impact on the floor, Khartov found it more difficult to breath

Chin pulled out his luggage and unzipped it. He produced a long white sheet. The men spread it over the carpeted floor and forcefully rolled Khartov onto it. She wanted to beg them to stop, to let her go, but no sound came from her mouth. She was completely nude, and the men were touching her, kissing her all over. She was completely helpless. But the rape was not the worst of it for her.

Khartov heard the men urging the one they called Darryl to rape her first. She was sobbing as the man named Darryl mounted her and took her. One by one, the men violated her. Her begging and pleas for mercy were not answered.

When the men finished violating her, Caine, Alexander and Jackson began the torture. Alexander cut off the tips of her fingers at the knuckles using large weapons similar to old gardening tools, with razor sharp blades. She screamed and screamed but no sound came out of her voice. As Alexander cut off her fingers, Caine used a small flame weapon and would burn the wound to stop the bleeding. The men laughed, as they heard her screaming courtesy of their radio receivers.

The pain was unbearable for Khartov. She wanted to pass out, but Stapler had injected her with something that prohibited her from doing so.

"She won't be able to pass out now," Stapler said, laughing. He had injected their victim with a mix of adrenaline concentrate and a drug known as Red Dust. The mixture would cause Khartov to feel the pain and prohibit her body's defense mechanisms, such as passing out from the pain, to occur. Her heart was racing, pounding in her chest like she had never felt.

Khartov had tears of pain rolling down her cheeks as she silently prayed for a miracle, that someone would come for her. She hoped that Les Gillis would come back for her. But, when Jackson pulled out his large knife and sliced off Khartov's left ear, she felt the searing pain of the cut, the ripping of the ear from her head, she knew that she was going to die tonight.

She felt her toes being severed by the same tool her attackers used on her fingers. She could hear the men laugh at her pain, celebrating how easy it was to take her life. One of the men stuck a knife into her left eye and pulled it from its eye socket. She heard the man brag that her eye was a souvenir.

Khartov saw from her remaining eye that one of the men had an axe in his hands. She screamed as the man chopped off both of her feet just above her ankles. Using hand held blow torch instruments the other men quickly burned the open wounds to prevent massive blood loss. The same ritual was repeated when they severed her hands just above the wrists and then her lower arms just above the elbow. She felt the stinging pain when Caine cut open her abdomen and began to pull out her intestines.

Khartov wanted death to come to her, but she had more torture to endure. Alexander began slicing her skin off of her upper arms, like an experience butcher would cut fat off of a prime cut of meat. The torture lasted thirty minutes, and eventually Khartov mercifully bled out internally and died.

"That was great!" Darryl said as he danced around Khartov's carcass.

Caine slapped his little brother on his shoulder. "Everyone get dressed. Lomax, fold the body pieces up in the DNA Absorption Mat. Let's get to the fifth floor where our second victim is waiting to meet her destiny."

Lomax and Chin began rolling the white DNA absorption mat up, with Khartov's butchered body inside. The white blanket created and manufactured by the Rosenburg Corporation, absorbed all of the blood and all of the DNA of the men's semen and sweat. Stapler and Alexander pulled out small aerosol cans and sprayed down the entire hotel room. The cans were also a creation of the Rosenburg's which would wipe out all finger prints, hair, sweat, semen, blood and saliva as if it was all being deleted from a computer. Eliminating finger prints and DNA traces of the men was as easy as pressing "delete" to remove an unwanted item on a computer.

When the cover up was completed, Lomax took the red rolling luggage and stuffed the DNA absorber with Khartov's body into it. "I have the ship on space number Seven Two Three at the docking bay. I will see you all there. Have fun with the next wench."

Lomax took the luggage with Khartov's carved body out of the room.

Caine looked at his group and his little brother. He was full of energy from the joy he felt from the rape and torture of the random woman. He wanted more action.

"Fifth floor gentlemen."

Drayton Love-Easter set his lit marijuana cigarette in his ash tray and leaned back in his chair. He pulled out his small Fenster Corporation hand held Holo-com device from his breast pocket. Over the years, he had recorded memorable moments on the electronic memory so he could relive those brief periods in time. Even though he was a tough graduate from Spetsnaz, deep down he was as sentimental as the next person. It was a side of his personality he rarely showed to others.

"Computer, show the recording of Yesenia at Lake Lynott." Love-Easter said softly. A year earlier, he had taken a weekend trip with his love, Yesenia, to Lynott's Land on New Edinburgh. The large Lake Lynott there was famous for the clear blue water, romantic cliffs, rolling hills and soft purple sand. There were still some flesh eating organisms in the water, so swimming was out of the question. But the view was both spectacular and romantic. It was one of the most wonderful times in Love-Easter's life.

The holographic three dimensional image of Yesenia Guevara in a bikini appeared before Love-Easter. She was waiving at him, smiling. She blew him a kiss. She had not been aware he was recording her.

"I love you Dray!" The image of Yesenia Guevara said, laughing.

He heard his reply of "I love you too, brown eyes!"

He watched as he chased her, both laughing. He watched their romantic kiss and felt her stomach. Love-Easter recalled that was the weekend she told him she was pregnant with their child. He wiped the tears from his eyes as he watched the recording of them holding each other and kissing romantically.

"God, I miss her so much," Love-Easter said as tears rolled down his cheeks.

The men followed Caine to the elevator lift. Darryl wanted to tell his brother and the others how great he felt after raping the stranger and helping cut her to pieces. He never felt so alive; it was as if his whole body was burning with excitement. His heart was pounding hard in his chest. Darryl could not wait to do the same to the Greek girl on the fifth floor.

The group, minus Lomax, moved rapidly down the fifth floor hallway. When they arrived at Papanikolaou's door, the men looked up and down the hallway and noted that there were no witnesses.

Inside the room, Elektra Papanikolaou was putting her hair up with two sharp pointed Corinthian metal hair holders. They were shaped like thin knives and perfect for a woman with long hair to twirl it and set her hair up. Each one was about a foot and a half in length. Papanikolaou thought she heard some footsteps outside her hotel doorway. She wondered if Frazier had come back to see if she changed her mind about him spending the night. She found herself smiling at the thought of the eventuality that she would be with Frazier. He was not macho, not pushy, but handsome, kind and very intelligent. She enjoyed his conversation regarding rocks and the process of extracting valuable gasses, oils and metals from the earth. Papanikolaou would never have believed that she would find herself attracted to a non-Greek man that was into rocks. Rocks of all things.

She hoped that it was Frazier she heard coming to her door.

"Arch," Papanikolaou called out loudly. "Is that you?"

She was facing the door when it suddenly burst open. She saw shocked to see two men charging at her, and neither was Arch Frazier. Papanikolaou stood up in a defensive posture and screamed as loud as she could.

Next door, Drayton Love-Easter heard the blood curdling scream. He was enjoying a fresh cup of coffee that room service had delivered along with a tasty Chicken Jerusalem and a Caesar salad. Love-Easter knew full well whose voice he heard. It was Elektra and she was in trouble! He jumped to his feet and grabbed the small four foot long metal club he always had with him when he traveled. He kept it for protection due to thieves, pirates and other criminal elements that were prevalent in the solar system. He ordered the computer to open the door and ran out into the hallway toward Elektra's door.

Love-Easter saw a strange Asian man standing at her door way. He was certain he had never seen the man before. Love-Easter did not hesitate and moved quickly toward the unknown man.

"Move out of the way!" Love-Easter ordered the man.

Chin smiled at Love-Easter. Good, Chin thought to himself, a challenge. Chin charged at Love-Easter and the two men began fighting. Love-Easter parried Chin's kicks, blocking them with his arms. Chin realized that his opponent was not the average man. He knew how to block his kicks with ease, suggesting that Chin's opponent had received some advanced training in the martial arts. Chin attempted to deliver a few karate blows at his opponent and had each attack blocked.

Chin was to learn quickly that his first impressions of Love-Easter were correct. Love-Easter went on the offensive and landed a few kicks into Chin's chest area, sending him stumbling backwards into the wall. Love-Easter knew he had to get to Elektra quickly. He did not have time to play with this man. Using his metal club, Love-Easter swung it at full strength and dispatched his opponent by connecting with Chin's skull. Chin cried out and spun toward the wall and smashed into it hard. Chin slid to the floor unconscious.

Love-Easter knew something was very wrong based on the limited evidence that he had. His friend had screamed, and her reputation was that of a tough young lady as opposed to the squeamish type, so her cry for help meant that she was in peril. The strange man guarding her door heightened his suspicions. He kicked Elektra's door twice before it cracked open. The door fell into another man; Love-Easter did not know who he was, sending him sprawling to the floor. Love-Easter saw Papanikolaou being held, a man gripping her right arm, another gripping her left. There was another man ripping the clothes off of her.

"Let her go!" Love-Easter ordered them.

Avery "Big Bad" Jackson had been in the restroom when he heard the door crash into Darryl Rosenburg. Alexander and Stapler were restraining the girl while Caine was stripping her. Jackson saw the strange man burst into the hotel room, holding a metal club. Jackson knew they had to abort the killing of the woman and get past this Good Samaritan to escape the space station security lock down that was certain to follow. Jackson pulled out his large knife and swung it at Love-Easter, slashing at his arm.

Love-Easter felt the knife cut into his right forearm. He was able to hold onto his club, thanks to the pain endurance training at Spetsnaz, which was clearly a valuable tool at this point. Love-Easter cursed himself for not being cognizant of the bathroom to his right. That was a rookie mistake, Love-Easter swore to himself. He stepped back as the large assailant lunged at him again. Love-Easter assessed that he needed room to maneuver to fight this bigger man. He moved backwards into the hallway. Love-Easter hoped the other three would lose interest in Elektra and pursue him. Jackson predictably followed Love-Easter out into the hallway, slashing his knife at him. Love-Easter avoided the slashes by side stepping the larger man's arms.

Caine cursed as he knew they had to leave the girl. They had broken the most important rule, never let the victim scream. Now there was going to be an investigation and two witnesses that could identify them. "Let's get out of here. Damn!"

Alexander and Stapler dropped their intended victim to the floor and rushed outside to help Jackson. They saw Love-Easter and Jackson swinging their weapons at one another. Love-Easter was bleeding from the gash in his upper right arm. They could tell the interloper was a well-trained fighter. Love-Easter hit Jackson in the jaw with his metal club. The crack of metal on bone was loud. Jackson staggered back, spitting out blood and pieces of busted teeth.

Alexander and Stapler also saw that Chin was on the ground.

Caine helped his brother to his feet, "Come on, we have to abort."

Caine saw Love-Easter run and kick Jackson in the chest. Jackson fell backwards into Stapler and both men hit the floor with a thud. Alexander had pulled out his knife and swirled around behind Love-Easter and cut him across the left side of his back. Love-Easter turned to face Alexander as Jackson and

Stapler picked themselves off the floor. Chin was also moving, slowly, as the Rosenburg brothers stood back and watched the fight. Caine knew this had to end quickly. Even his sister would not be able to cover this mess up. Caine reached into his cargo pants pocket and pulled out a Rosenburg hand laser, stun model 755. He struggled to get a good shot at Love-Easter, as Alexander, Jackson and Stapler kept getting in the way of his aim.

At the moment he thought he had a good shot, Caine was shoved to the ground by Papanikolaou. She had thrown on a long t-shirt to cover herself and decided to lend Love-Easter a hand. Caine rolled to the floor and looked up at Papanikolaou and observed that she was gritting her teeth and had fire in her eyes. She pulled out her two large metal hair braces and held one in each hand as if they were knives. Darryl watched the woman shove his brother to the floor and determined that this was his chance to prove his worth to his older brother. Darryl backhanded Papanikolaou before she could press her attack on Caine. Papanikolaou did not react as Darryl thought. She did not run away crying as many women had when the Rosenburg men abused them. This woman was different. She was a fighter.

Papanikolaou turned her fury at Darryl, growling as she jumped at him. On the floor, Caine watched helplessly as the woman stabbed both blades into Darryl's chest. The younger Rosenburg screamed out loud. One of the thin blades pierced his left lung and the other blade sank into his muscle on his right side. The pain from the two wounds caused Darryl to collapse to the ground with blood leaking out onto his shirt. His eyes were staring helplessly at his brother Caine.

Love-Easter suffered several more cuts on his back and chest by Alexander and Jackson. But he had been trained to fight and ignore pain. Love-Easter hit Stapler on his right upper arm with his metal club. Stapler cried out and stumbled out of the way. Love-Easter kicked with his right foot and connected with Alexander in the chest.

Caine desperately kicked Papanikolaou against the wall. He turned and finally had an opening for a clean shot at Love-Easter. He fired a blast from his hand laser. The yellow beam connected with Love-Easter in his back. The stunned Love-Easter fell face first to the floor.

Jackson and Alexander quickly pounced on Love-Easter with their knives ready. They began stabbing the unconscious man relentlessly. Alexander grabbed Love-Easter's hair and pulled his head back and slashed his throat open.

Papanikolaou was struggling to get back on her feet and watched helplessly as the men were stabbing Love-Easter. When they moved to cut his throat, she screamed: "NO!"

Alexander dropped Love-Easter to the floor, his blood gushing out onto the carpet from his severed jugular vein. The men were now free to eliminate their final witness. They began to turn their attention toward Papanikolaou when the elevator doors at the end of the hall opened. Yuri Gorski, Jen Staszko,

Les Gillis and Michel Evart entered the hallway.

Papanikolaou saw her friends in the distance. "Thank Hera! Yuri! They killed Drayton!"

Gorski and his friends looked over the scene. Love-Easter was lying on the blood stained floor and he was not moving. There was blood all over the floors and walls. Papanikolaou had a bruise on her cheek. The other combatants were all strangers to Gorski and his friends. Gorski growled and began running full speed at the attackers, the others close behind.

Caine turned toward the woman that had stabbed Darryl and fired his laser pistol at her. Papanikolaou cried out as she slumped to the ground. Caine knew the situation was rapidly growing out of control. Now there were witnesses to everything. They had to retreat to the back security halls of the Baroness and make for their escape from the space station.

Jackson snarled and met Gorski in the center of the hallway, swinging his knife at the new opponent. Gorski dodged several knife slashes by stepping backwards and then to his right. Jen Staszko pulled out her four inch long throwing knives from her boots. She threw one them with her right hand, hitting the Asian man in his left shoulder. Her blade went all the way through, almost to the hilt. Chin screamed in pain as the blade sunk into his flesh and muscle.

Gillis ran at full speed and tackled Alexander. As the two men hit the floor, Gillis began punching the man in his ribs and abdomen. Gillis was hitting the man so hard he knocked Alexander's breath out of him. Alexander felt one of his ribs break. Gillis kept hitting the man, filled with rage at seeing his best friend lying in blood on the floor.

Evart jumped into the air and drop kicked Stapler, sending him rolling to the ground. Stapler rolled to avoid Evart's next kick. Stapler leaped to his feet and engaged Evart in hand to hand combat. The two men began exchanging punches and kicks, each giving equal punishment to the other.

Many of the other patrons on the fifth floor of the Baroness Hotel heard the screams and the sound of laser fire. There were now several witnesses watching from their doorways, but none were brave enough to enter the deadly combat in the hallway. They stood back with fear in their eyes. Some were gasping at the violent scene. The vast majority of civilians were terrified to get involved at all for fear of reprisals from the perpetrators or their own government.

"Someone call security!" Evart barked at the civilian audience. He did not wait to see if anyone followed his demand and continued his fight with Stapler.

Gorski grabbed Jackson's knife arm and swung it downward onto his knee. Jackson's arm cracked and he screamed more out of anger than pain. He dropped his blade as Gorski twisted his injured arm. Jackson punched Gorski in the face with his free hand. Jackson was breathing heavily and grinding his teeth. Jackson wanted to kill this man. "You broke my arm!" He lunged at Gorski who sidestepped him and kicked the much larger man in the groin.

Caine checked his little brother, Darryl. The two slender hair blades in his chest were causing substantial loss of blood. Caine knew they had to get medical help quickly or Darryl would bleed to death.

Caine turned toward the fight and noticed that he had a clear shot at the red headed man and fired at him. Gillis did not see the yellow laser hit him but felt the electrical charge surge through his body and he fell to the floor. With Gillis out, Alexander was free to help elsewhere and he turned to Evart and kicked the Frenchman's legs out from under him. Evart felt the breath get knocked out of him when he hit the ground.

Staszko threw her last knife at the man with the laser and her aim was true, the knife slicing into Caine's lower left arm. Caine screamed and dropped his laser. "Run!"

His men complied, running for the elevator. Jackson shoved Gorski out of the way. Realizing that she could not stop the charging men, Staszko jumped against the wall. They were carrying Darryl, who was struggling to breathe. Staszko ran for Love-Easter and she checked for a pulse.

They were too late. He was dead. Staszko began crying, cradling her dear friend's head in her lap.

Gorski barked at some of the curious tenants to call security as he checked Papanikolaou and determined she was only stunned. Evart had recovered and checked on Gillis.

Gorski ran to where Staszko was holding Love-Easter. Gorski saw the blood all over the walls and the floor. He knew his friend was dead just by the amount of blood. Gorski slammed his right fist into the wall in anger. They were too late to save him.

CHAPTER EIGHT

Lieutenant Garrison arrived at the crime scene on the fifth floor of the Baroness Hotel after having his sleep disturbed by the rude computer notification. He stood back at first, observing that it was already bustling. Several Criminal Investigation Division agents were already present, in plain clothes, interviewing the witnesses. In the room of the decedent were the survivors of the attack. Garrison could hear the constant sobbing of one of the women victims. The body of Drayton Love-Easter was on the floor and two female medical pathologists were examining his wounds. Other law enforcement officers were present taking photographs of the blood splatters, the broken door and taking fingerprints off of the contents in the room. Garrison saw spatters of blood on the ceiling, walls and floor. The scene looked like an artist took cans of red paint and tossed it against the walls.

Detective Charles Bennington, the lead Criminal Investigation Division officer at the scene, recognized Garrison and approached him. Bennington was fifty-eight years old and had retired several years ago from the Space Command Military Intelligence as a Colonel. Over the over three decades of military service that Bennington gave he had seen many crime scenes and was involved in several instances of combat. The position of C.I.D. lead detective on Space Station Cy-7 came available and Bennington applied, finding retirement boring. He was hired immediately.

"Lieutenant, I ordered a lock down of the entire space station," Bennington told Garrison, whispering. "Three ships, all private transports, left before we could close the bulkheads. I have asked Military Intelligence to trace the ships down using the serial numbers they had registered with when they docked."

Garrison nodded. Everything was going as criminal investigative procedure required.

Bennington continued whispering to Garrison. "The victim here was a senior at Clovis Academy. He was twenty-two years old and was a recent graduate of the Spetsnaz Special Forces training. He was one tough hombre to bring down. And he is the oldest son of that revival preacher on the three dimensional broadcasts, Pastor Love-Easter."

Hearing the name caused Garrison's blood to run cold. Garrison realized that soon there would be an onslaught of news reporters swarming the station. Any time a high profile murder occurred, it attracted the news media like vultures. "I will instruct all of the security personnel to make no comments to the news media. How about the security scanners from the Hotel offices? Were we able to make any positive identifications as to the perpetrators from those computer print outs?"

Bennington leaned in closer to Garrison; his eyes looked around the room suspiciously. "It would seem that the Hotel Manager, Penelope Smith, noticed that the security scanners were disabled during the time the crime was committed. She was here earlier with two nurses and her chief of security, an Ella Ragnarsson. Both of the women were interviewed and they went back to their jobs with the Hotel. I would be careful with them. I think they are hiding something."

Garrison raised his eyebrows since he had the same uneasiness in the manner the two women interacted with him. "An inside job?"

"I am a suspicious man and the women seemed evasive to my questioning. It is also quite the coincidence that all monitors are off line during the commission of a homicide. We will follow the leads as to the missing space craft, just in case, and interview everyone on the space station. But as of now, no one leaves this hotel. My staff of investigators and DNA experts will be doing life form scans to determine if there are any possible suspects hiding in wash rooms, closets, or other crevices. The entire management staff of the Hotel is under suspicion."

"Which is why we are whispering," Garrison stepped over to the body. "I will need to interview the surviving victims."

A female DNA technician pointed to Love-Easter's hotel room and Garrison walked in the open doorway to see Papanikolaou on the bed sobbing. Garrison did not realize that the woman was to the point of being hysterical with guilt, blaming herself for Love-Easter's death. Staszko had her arms around the distraught girl, trying in vain to give her comfort. Gillis was sitting on the floor staring blankly at the far wall, his eyes still red from fighting back the emotions of losing his best friend. Evart was sitting on the black leather couch with a similar blank look on his face, trying to think of who would want to hurt his friends. Gorski was pacing back and forth. Garrison thought Gorski was like a caged tiger that wanted to go hunting.

"Why? They didn't have to kill him!" Papanikolaou was sobbing. "Dray was stunned. He was out cold." The poor girl was looking at Staszko for answers. "Dray wasn't even a threat to them. Why? Why?" She kept repeating the question.

"Not you again," Garrison said when he recognized Gorski and Staszko.

The anger on Gorski's face was evident as he walked over to Garrison. "Lieutenant, there were six of them. They murdered our friend. They tried to rape Elektra. Dray jumped in to defend her and they killed him for it!"

Garrison held his hands up, palms toward Gorski, "Calm down kid. Our entire C.I.D. is on it. My security marines have sealed off the station and no one is getting off this station until we catch these killers and arrest them."

Gorski kept pacing back and forth, "What about the security tapes? Those should have given you a positive identification as to the murderers. Take their images to the computer imaging programs and you will know who did this."

Garrison shook his head at Gorski's suggestion, "For some reason the security scanners were not in operation at the time of the attack. I need for the five of you come with me to the security section for complete statements. We will also each of you to all give us detailed descriptions of the perpetrators. But right now I need you to tell me whether or not any of the six attackers were injured?"

Papanikolaou spoke up when she heard that question, "Yes sir. I stabbed one of them in the chest with my Corinthian hair clips. I stabbed him twice. He was a young white man. Dark eyes." Her voice was filled with pride that she had been able to hurt one of the attackers.

Garrison turned to the young girl, "Forgive me for being an ignorant man, how does one stab a person with hair clips?

"They were sharp metal rods," Staszko answered for her friend. "They are made in Corinth on Earth. You spin your hair around the rod and pin the hair up."

Garrison nodded, understanding.

Gorski spoke up next, "The Asian attacker was stabbed in the arm. The Anglo male using the hand laser was stabbed in the lower right arm. The tall black man had some busted teeth and I broke one of his arms."

Garrison pulled his small Holo-com device out of his breast pocket, "Docking security, this is Garrison. Look for six attackers, four were injured. One white male was stabbed twice in the chest. Another white male should have a knife wound on his lower right arm. There is a very tall dark man with broken teeth and a broken arm. Also there is an Asian male with a knife wound in his arm. Send teams to the two medical clinics to follow these leads. Also, alert New Edinburgh Security in case the perpetrators fled to the planet surface and try to seek out medical assistance. Have them check out all of the medical clinics and hospitals."

"Yes sir," Came the response from a female operative.

Garrison motioned to the door, "Please, follow me. We will go to the security station for your statements. Then you need to have our psychiatrist interview you for emotional trauma counseling."

Gillis slowly rose to his feet feeling numb inside from the horrific event. Love-Easter had been his roommate in the Academy Dormitory for almost four years. They had been as close as brothers, sharing outlines, studying together, carousing and partying at the campus bars. Love-Easter had always been so positive and insightful. He had been a man that Gillis could confide in, even with his most secret thoughts, without any fear that those secrets would be shared with others. He was stunned that his closest friend was killed in such a manner. His thoughts were racing trying to recall anyone that would have wanted to cause Love-Easter's death. Gillis could think of no one. Other than the occasional bar fight, Love-Easter was liked by all of their classmates.

As they walked out of the room, they passed by the body of Love-Easter. Papanikolaou began to sob again.

CHAPTER NINE

The private space craft had barely escaped the space station when the security bulk heads began to close. Lomax had proven to be an effective pilot as he flew low enough to the docking bay to just make it under the closing metal bulk heads. Lomax had helped Caine carry in his dying brother, Darryl, as the other injured members of the group loaded on board. Lomax knew the security protocol and immediately fired the engines up and blasted off.

Caine held his brother in his arms, listening to each of the younger mans labored breaths for air. He was not going to make it back to the medical doctors at Rosenburg's Ranch. The others took pain killers and patched their own wounds. Chin used a hand laser to cauterize his own arm and stop the bleeding.

The escape from the Baroness Hotel had been difficult. The men ran to the security corridor while carrying Darryl. Caine had to order his sister Penelope to have the hotel security eliminate the blood trail from the fifth floor to the offices. Using the back hallways, Caine led the group to a secret entrance to the docking area where their ship was waiting.

Caine held his brother as Alexander injected Darryl with a pain killer. The young Darryl smiled at Caine, "We made it. We got away."

"Don't talk, save your strength," Caine told him.

Darryl was looking at the ceiling of the space craft. "I had the time of my life." His head fell to the side and he sighed. His breathing stopped.

Caine felt Darryl's neck for a pulse and found none. Caine laid the body of Darryl on the cold metal floor of the space craft. He stood and walked to an observation window, staring out into space, watching Space Station Cy-7 grow smaller as the distance between her and the escape ship grew. Caine checked the gash in his right arm and cursed the Clovis Academy woman with the knives. If she and the three other men had not shown up they might have been able to escape and get medical attention for Darryl. Caine walked over to Jackson, Chin, Alexander and Stapler. Chin had stopped the bleeding from his wound on his own. Jackson was holding his broken arm; his cheeks were puffed up from his broken teeth. Alexander was grimacing with pain and holding his rib cage with both arms.

"Darryl's dead," Caine told them bluntly. "My sister will cover up all evidence of this, so we will get away with it...."

Jackson cut him off, pointing his left index finger in his

face. "I don't give a damn! That bastard broke my arm! Nobody does this to me! Nobody! I want blood."

Stapler nodded in agreement, "We all want blood. That Greek bitch saw all of us. She can identify us. Once she gives out our descriptions, we will get arrested. They will find us."

Caine shook his head, "Not to worry, there will be no arrests. My family has contacts and all of the power in the eight solar systems. We will never be found out. We all go about life as normal. Let the heat die down and after enough time has passed by, we will get blood. We kill them all when they least expect it. But we do it my way. Understood?"

Chin nodded and Stapler grudgingly agreed. Alexander stood up, cussing. Jackson glared at the other men, his nostrils flaring with rage. "When we do kill them, I want the son of a bitch that broke my arm. He's mine!"

Yuri Gorski sat down at a large metal desk across from a Criminal Investigation Detective. The headquarters of the investigators was two levels above the Hotel and about a kilometer walk in distance. Gorski led his friends in silence to the CID offices so that each could give their statements and help with the apprehension of the murderers.

Les Gillis felt as if he were in a nightmare and could not wake up. He was sitting at a large desk across from a plain clothed detective with the Criminal Investigation Division. The detective was named Papalbon. Gillis noted that Papalbon was about sixty years old, had a large belly, double chin, grey hair and his breath smelled as if he had not brushed his teeth in a week. Gillis believed that if this Papalbon was in the prestigious C.I.D., then the famed investigatory agency was not worthy of its' stellar reputation.   Gillis answered many questions propounded by Papalbon. Some were routine, others were probing into the subject of who would want the victim dead. Gillis was insulted when he was asked by Papalbon whether he and his friends killed Love-Easter and made up the story of the six attackers.

Gillis stood up and was yelling at the detective, pointing his finger at him. "You worthless fat slob! My friend is dead! Dead! And you think you are going to solve the case making baseless accusations! Turn in your badge!"

Gorski had to excuse himself from where he was sitting and run to Gillis in an effort to calm him down. "Les, they are just doing their jobs. Just answer his questions. Please."

Gillis looked into Gorski's eyes. The trust between the two men was unshakeable. Gillis nodded his head and slowly sat back down in his chair. He looked at Detective Papalbon and said: "No. Hell no. I did not kill my best friend. And no, my friends here did not kill him either."

Papalbon continued asking other questions of Gillis such as Love-Easter's personal life, women he had been involved with, any rivals on campus that might have a grudge against him. Gillis did as Gorski instructed and answered each and every question given to him.

After three hours of interrogation, Yuri Gorski and his friends finished their statements to the investigators. Papanikolaou gave detailed descriptions of her attackers. She had been able to compose herself long enough to assist the officers as best she could. Garrison took the descriptions and gave them to computer artists in his security section. Garrison told two of his security marines to escort Gorski and the group to the medical center for physical and psychiatric treatment. Garrison had concluded that the cadets were not his perpetrators as they were all cooperating fully with the authorities and their stories all matched. They wanted Drayton's killers caught and brought to justice. Garrison was impressed at the level of loyalty the Academy students had toward the victim. Garrison watched them leave his office and it was then he received the notification to report to the captain's command booth. He received the order in a hand written piece of paper from a U.N.S.C. Technical Sergeant named Olivo.

Garrison read the note that was from the Captain of the space station which ordering him to report immediately to the command central headquarters. Garrison followed Olivo out into the main hallway of Cy-7 and they walked for over a kilometer until they approached the security restricted elevator entrance. Only space station Cy-7 section commanders and their ranking non-commissioned officers were cleared to use that specific elevator. It was a security precaution that the Space Command security had dreamed up decades ago.

Garrison and Olivo entered the elevator after Garrison's palm print cleared the computer security scans. The elevator shot off, sideways first, to the center of the space station. Once there the elevator began rising to the upper levels of the command offices. After the elevator stopped the doors slid open.

Garrison followed Olivo into the Command Booth.

The Command Booth was a circular room that was three levels high. There were observation windows around the top with a spectacular view of New Edinburgh. There were metal steps and levels above with computer banks and some technicians walking back and forth, checking readings on oxygen levels, orbiting information, solar panel effectiveness. The technicians had to conduct safety inspections every hour on the hour. A few engineers were checking panels as well, ensuring there were no warning signs on the mechanical operations of the station.

The lower level of the Command Booth had a few desks with computers. Around the desks were several plush, black couches. Sitting in the couches Garrison saw CID investigator Charles Bennington, Hotel Baroness Manager Penelope Smith (Rosenburg), Army Command Sergeant Major Karam, Captain of the space station Wallace Traxler and a woman unknown to Garrison.

Sergeant Major Karam was sixty-three years old. His service to the Empire had been extensive. Only his left leg was his natural limb. He had lost his arms and right leg in different combat missions over the decades. The lost arms and legs had been replaced by life-like mechanical appendages that were covered with real human skin. He had not retired as he seemed to enjoy the quiet and calm workload aboard the space station as the top non-commissioned officer. Captain Traxler had served for several years as a captain on a Battle Cruiser. He commanded several missions into hostile events and served with distinction. On three occasions, he had been passed over for promotion to Admiral. He finally applied for transfer to captain a space station and was assigned the Cy-7. Traxler was bitter toward the Security Council military advisors for not recommending him for admiral. But, as a good commander will often do, he hid his bitterness and always spoke in a positive manner regarding the service.

In the center of the room was a three dimensional image of three star General Gerald Welker. Garrison knew that something was amiss to bring in one of the top ranking officers of the Space Command to a meeting. General Welker was one of the top ranking Generals in the Earth Empire's Military Intelligence. In addition, Welker was the grandson of the Earth Empire's Glorious Leader, Secretary General Vladimir Sikorsky. Garrison was concerned that the fact that there was a member of the Royal Family attending this meeting meant that the death of the preacher's son was being scrutinized by the Glorious Leader himself. The image of Welker was of a young man wearing his solid black Class A uniform with three gold stars on each shoulder. Welker should have been a man of at least one hundred seventy years of age, but he looked no older than forty years old.

Traxler noticed that Garrison had arrived and stood up, "Have a seat, Lieutenant. General, everyone involved is now present."

Garrison sat down on the couch next to the woman he knew as Penelope Smith. She was wearing a low-cut white blouse, exposing some cleavage, and a skin tight black mini-skirt. He smiled at her and studied her for any imperfections. He concluded that the manager of the Hotel Baroness was too perfect. Her face, eye lashes, her full lips, curvaceous body, long perfect legs were all perfect. A woman that looked that amazing should be in the movies, not managing a hotel hidden on a random space station, he thought to himself.

"Good," General Welker said. "Now, will someone give me an update on the murder investigation that you are all involved in?"

Garrison looked to Bennington to determine which of the two men would speak first. This was General Welker, and every word had to be carefully thought out. Before either man could stand and speak, the woman that Garrison had never met before stood up. She walked toward the three dimensional view of the General. She was a tall, attractive blonde in her late twenties. She had blue eyes, long legs and full lips. She was wearing a black business suit and was carrying a large black leather bag over her right shoulder.

"General, my name is Ella Ragnarsson," The woman introduced herself. "I am the security director for the Baroness Hotel. My staff and I were the first on the scene of the murder on the fifth floor of our hotel. We alerted the CID and station security immediately after we secured the crime scene. We secured both hotel rooms of the victims and searched them thoroughly. We also searched and secured the fifth floor hallway. Our investigation has been able to turn up the identity of the assailant."

Garrison was confused by her statement and spoke up, "The assailant?" He put the emphasis on the "the." Ragnarsson gave him a dirty look but Garrison continued, "The witnesses said there was more than one."

"Let her finish, Lieutenant." Welker said sharply.

Garrison knew that was his cue to keep his mouth shut.

"We found evidence of both legal and illegal drugs in the hotel room of the murder victim," Ragnarsson continued. "Love-Easter had several marijuana cigarettes and packets of Red Dust, which we all know is a hyper potent psychedelic synthetic drug and is illegal. We found trace evidence of marijuana residue in the hotel room of Papanikolaou."

"And the medical examination concluded that Love-Easter had marijuana and Red Dust in his system," Bennington added from his chair.

"And we found weapons in both hotel rooms," Ragnarsson reported. "The woman had knives and a hand laser and Love-Easter also had the same types of weaponry. The hand lasers were military issued which would mean that these cadets illegally brought those weapons to the space station. It would also account for the laser fire heard by the witnesses."

Ragnarsson opened her black bag and pulled out a plastic bag with a large, blood stained knife inside. "We recovered this weapon in the hallway. DNA testing suggests it was the murder weapon. In addition, we found further DNA traces of the possible perpetrator. We ran the DNA results through the criminal justice data base and got a match."

Bennington took that as his time to speak, "General, the computer search revealed that the killer was a man named Alexi Khartov. He has warrants for his arrest on the Martian colonies, planet Cootron and Sikorsky's Planet for multiple murders, multiple rapes, felony assault and felony fraud."

Welker nodded, "Good work. Have we apprehended this Alexi Khartov?"

"Yes," Bennington answered. "He actually came to us. When we initiated the lock down of the space station, Khartov approached our security personnel looking for his wife, an Alejandra Khartov. While the space station staff attempted to assist Khartov in locating his wife, we received the report that Khartov was the killer we were looking for."

"Just one killer?" Garrison could not keep his silence any longer. "The other cadets that came to Papanikolaou's aid said there were at least six attackers. How could this Khartov take out a well-trained Spetsnaz graduate all alone?"

Ragnarsson seemed to have been anticipating the question, "You mean a stoned on illegal drugs Spetsnaz graduate, don't you? We believe that Khartov was paying Papanikolaou for sex and Love-Easter was jealous. He went into a drug induced rage and fought Khartov. The girl got her stun laser and shot Love-Easter. Khartov then cut the man's throat. She then stuns herself to cover up her involvement."

Garrison suddenly stood up, unable to contain his anger, "That is ridiculous. The cadets showed up and fought the killers. There were several different types of blood found at the crime scene. There were several different DNA types in the blood stains. The crime scene matched up with the story given to me and my security team. I believe we are looking for six attackers, not one."

There was an uncomfortable silence following his outburst. Ragnarsson finally spoke, "We all decided, Lieutenant Garrison, before you arrived, that those cadets could not be trusted."

"Come again?" Garrison asked.

"Yes. Each of your witnesses has had numerous accounts of Academy disciplinary code violations," Ragnarsson told them. "Yuri Gorski has been written up seventeen times by Dean Harvard and other professors at the Academy. He has been a one student wrecking machine complete with numerous bar fights and fights on campus. One time he stole a Raumschiff to fly a girl he was trying to impress and orbit around the planet for sex. Gorski has assembled a group of students that are the biggest trouble makers in this part of the solar system. Some of them were arrested a few years ago on Lynott's Land during a riot at a wedding."

"But, they did not display those personality traits to me." Garrison protested. "The girl was very upset and it was no act. I don't believe she would have done what you are saying."

"Really?" Ragnarsson asked. "Did you not arrest all of them last night for a bar fight?"

"The bar fight at Tinkerbelle's was not their fault," Garrison defended the cadets. "They were protecting a girl in danger. Plus, two of the other cadets that were witnesses to the murder did not participate in the Tinkerbelle bar fight. And then the other hotel guests on the fifth floor? What about them?"

Ragnarsson walked over to Garrison, "We also interviewed the hotel patrons and they gave statements that support my conclusions. And the other two cadets? Lester Brey Gillis is straight 'A' student. But his family still celebrates the Irish Republic on Earth. His entire family is a pack of rebels. Gillis himself has been involved in several of those disciplinary write-ups that Gorski started. Gillis also was sharing the same dormitory room with Love-Easter. Gillis would never say a bad word against the deceased. Are we really going to believe him?

"And Evart?" Ragnarsson continued. "He betrayed his family by leaving them behind and their restaurant business that had been in their family for many generations. Evart has no loyalties except to Gorski and Gillis and Love-Easter. Evart was also involved in the disciplinary actions of the others. His word cannot be trusted. And the other woman, Staszko? She came from a family of gypsies that travel around the Eastern European provinces of Hungary, Rumania, Bulgaria and Czechoslovakia. Her family is a bunch of thieves and con artists. No, Lieutenant Garrison. Their words mean nothing."

"So then it is settled," Welker announced. "Alexi Khartov was the lone assassin and it was a lover's quarrel gone badly. Captain Traxler, please send out the press release to the media via computer broadcast."

"Yes, General. Right away." Traxler promised.

"I don't need to tell all of you how important it is that this meeting remains private," Welker ordered. "The dead cadet came from a prominent religious leader's family. But since the family disowned him, the drug induced lovers argument will resonate with the Pastor. Garrison and Bennington, I need you to retain custody of the Clovis Academy cadets for a few days so we can keep them from the news media. Arrest them for two days."

"Sir, they have classes and training Monday morning," Garrison stated.

Welker raised his voice due to the insolence of anyone questioning his orders. "This is a matter of security, Lieutenant! Love-Easter's family potentially has billions of followers.

Billions with a B! We need to sell this version of the facts! If the Pastor and his flock sense any holes or mishandling of this investigation, they will literally raise hell!   So, Lieutenant Garrison, are you on board with us or not?"

Garrison, believing that his career hung on the next words out of his mouth, said the only thing that he could. "Yes, General. I am on board. You can count on me, Sir."

"Good," Welker said. "Tell the cadets they need to be held for their own protection. Tell them anything to keep them here without asking questions. And get a confession out of Alexi Khartov. One way or another. Do you understand?"

"Yes sir," Garrison said.

The image of General Welker disappeared.

"That went quite well." Captain Traxler said.

Bennington thanked Penelope Smith and Ella Ragnarsson for their assistance in the investigation. The two women left with Technical Sergeant Olivo.

Garrison finally turned to Bennington, "Are you okay with this?"

Bennington moved in closer to Garrison, "You need to learn when to shut the hell up. There is something big going on here. Bigger than you or me. We need to get behind this. These are powerful people, Garrison. I had a long career in the Space Command service before switching to CID. If a member of the Sikorsky family says jump, then you better ask how high. People that disobey have a nasty habit of having fatal accidents."

Garrison knew that the older man was correct. The Sikorsky regime had a well-deserved reputation for cruelty and brutality when it came to preserving their power. Garrison decided to take Bennington's advice and keep his opinions to himself, or he could end up dead. Or worse.

CHAPTER TEN

Lomax skillfully landed the space shuttle at the Rosenburg Ranch. The sky was still dark but the private landing strip was illuminated with many solar powered lights. Lomax saw a group of approximately thirty people waiting at the landing pad. He recognized one of the faces in the crowd as Caine's father. Lomax swallowed hard as he wondered how they would tell the man that his son Darryl died attempting to rape an innocent woman.

Lomax had been around many cruel people in his lifetime. As a child he had been the victim of child abuse and sexual abuse from his step-father. His mother would reject his outcries and would call him a liar. Lomax realized at that young age that he had to fend for himself. Lomax learned to find a place in his mind to escape the terrors when the man would corner him or visit him at night for sex. He was present in the physical as he was receiving the abuse, but he had trained his mind to focus on other subjects. He lived in fear of his step-father for years until his sixteenth birthday. Lomax waited for his step-father to come to his room, as he always did. He murdered his step-father by stabbing him repeatedly with a screwdriver. Lomax was convicted of murder as his mother convinced the prosecution that there had never been any sexual abuse in her home, sent away to a juvenile facility and spent three years learning anger management skills and fighting off gang rapes in the showers. No one would believe that the young teenage boy had been the victim of such brutal treatment at the hands of the step-father.

In the juvenile system, Lomax met other scary people that left their mark on his life. But there was no person that Lomax feared more than Alfred Rosenburg, II. Lomax had witnessed the elder Rosenburg lose his temper in the past. Rosenburg would kill without rhyme or reason. Now with a son dead, Lomax dreaded the reaction of the man when given the news.

The Rosenburg Ranch was located on the North Continent of New Edinburgh. The family was granted the property by the United Nations Security Council when New Edinburgh was being settled. Alfred Rosenburg, Senior, transferred his entire family leaving the Martian colony and Earth behind. The land mass that was granted to the Rosenburg's was as large as the former states of Texas and New Mexico combined. There were lakes and several rivers running through the vast land. Much of the property could be utilized as farm land. There were rolling hills, one mountain range at the border of the property line and manmade water wells that tapped into natural underground aquifers. Most of the Rosenburg Ranch was virgin forest area where they grew food, grains, and drugs.

The senior Rosenburg, his wife and two of his sons died in a dinosaur attack a few years after settling on the Ranch. The funeral service for Alfred Rosenburg, Senior was a Who's Who of the most rich and powerful in the Earth Empire. The Glorious Leader, Secretary General of the United Nations Security Council, Vladimir Sikorsky, attended. Many believed that Sikorsky was paying homage to a dead captain of industry. But, the hidden secret was that Alfred Rosenburg Senior was the grandson of Vladimir Sikorsky.

The property was inherited by the two living sons, Alfred Rosenburg, II and John Rosenburg. They shared in the management of the family business and the large land mass given to them. John Rosenburg had married twice in his lifetime. His first wife died in an accidental space craft collision. He remarried several years later to a woman twenty years younger than he was. John and his family occasionally lived in separate housing from Alfred. For the majority of the time, John and his family lived on Sikorsky's Planet working on secret projects for the Glorious Leader. There was the occasional family gathering in which the two brothers and their children would interact.

Lomax knew all of this history, as Caine had related to him during a late night, drunken conversation. Due to this knowledge, Lomax was also privy to the deviant behavior he could experience at the Rosenburg Ranch. When Lomax opened the bay doors several slaves, guards, employees and a shrieking woman jumped on board the ship. The woman was Francesca Powers Rosenburg. She was forty-nine years old, but due to the harvested body parts of younger women, Francesca looked twenty. Francesca had been born into a family that had been financially powerful for several centuries. The Powers family had owned many clothing and department retail sales locations. During one of the economic depressions, her family business, which was being run by fifth generation offspring of the original Powers family, ran into massive debt. Alfred Rosenburg, II, had learned of the near financial ruin of the Powers family business and loaned them a considerable sum of money to keep the Powers retail operation afloat. One of Rosenburg's demands was that they would supply one of their family members to become one of his wives to bear him more children. Francesca was given to Rosenburg as part of the interest on the loans. She had been fifteen years old at the time of the arrangement. Francesca had given birth to several children during her marriage to Alfred. Her youngest son had been Darryl. After searching the space shuttle frantically, Francesca found Darryl's body on the floor of the space ship. She kept screaming over and over, "My baby!"

Avery "Big Bad" Jackson wanted to stab her to shut her up, but knew that would only get him killed. He despised wailing women, except when he was raping or torturing them.

Alfred Rosenburg slowly ascended the ramp to the space ship. He moved like a young man in his twenties, but everyone knew that Alfred was one hundred seventy-seven years old. He had been kept young by having vital organs replaced by harvesting those body parts from young men and women. Many had died to keep Alfred alive. His skin had been replaced five times. His brain patterns, at age eighty seven, had been downloaded to a computer chip and Alfred took the brain of a young intellectual for his own. Alfred's entire memory was downloaded into the younger man's brain and placed in his metallic skull.

Alfred had been informed by one of his daughters, Penelope, that one of his sons had been killed. Penelope had made it clear that Caine had been the reason for the death. Walking just a few steps behind Alfred was another one of his other wives, Magdalena. Magdalena had also kept herself young by using the computer technology and harvested body parts. Magdalena was Caine's biological mother and currently Alfred's favorite spouse. Father and mother approached Caine.

"What the hell happened? Caine! Explain this!" Alfred demanded.

"A guy caught us because the girl screamed before we could gag her and..." Caine began stammering. Caine was terrified of his father's wrath.

But Caine was even more loathe to the form of punishment he would receive from his mother. In years past, Magdalena had been a hired killer for the Rosenburg family. She had killed dozens of people in cold blood. Magdalena enjoyed her work and had been the one to convince father to kill his older brother, Cush. Caine had watched his mother murder a male slave that had been rude enough to forget to bring the proper amount of ice cubes for her drink. He recalled watching as Magdalena impaled an ice pick into the doomed man's left eye socket for his momentary lapse in memory. Magdalena merely stated as the man was dying, "He will never forget again." Caine's father had married Magdalena to keep her talent for assassination on the side of the Rosenburg family.

"Shut the hell up!" His father yelled at him. "We had to call in favors from high up. This kind of stuff is what gets us caught! We must keep a low profile you cretin!" The elder Rosenburg backhanded Caine across the face.

Caine looked down at the ground, his face stinging with pain. "I am sorry father."

"For what? Getting caught or getting your little brother killed?" The senior Rosenburg demanded while shaking his fist at him.

"Both," Caine responded. "I thought the plan was flawless."

Magdalena walked in circles around Caine, "I taught you

better. How could you think you could kill two women in a busy hotel and not be observed? Are you that stupid? If you are going to do such things, pick targets that are alone and in areas where the chance of being seen are minimal." There was contempt in her voice. She dared not consider what could happen if the rest of humanity knew of the body harvesting that the Rosenburg's and Sikorsky's had been involved with over the last two centuries. The results of calling attention to any of their activities could lead to demands for resignations, riots, and even planetary or multi planetary civil war. She was furious at Caine for his stupidity and recklessness.

"I know mother, I know. I am so sorry." Caine said, watching the employees carry Darryl's body from the ship with his wailing mother, Francesca, following behind them.

"So, what are you going to do about getting justice for Darryl?" Magdalena demanded. Whenever a Royal Family member was killed there had to be reprisals. Otherwise one death would encourage more killings. As the Royal Family saying went, weakness is provocative.

Caine shrugged, "I don't know. I hadn't thought of anything yet."

Magdalena grabbed Caine's right arm, where his knife wound was, and squeezed her fingernails into his wound. Caine screamed in agony and fell to his knees. "You are too pathetic to be my son!" Magdalena told him. "Your father and I have some ideas. Get your friends ready to transport out. Go back to

Achilles Academy. You are to do nothing. Nothing! We will let you know what to do and when to do it!"

Caine had tears running down his cheeks, "Yes mother. I'll do nothing. I will wait for you and father for the next step."

Magdalena released his arm. Caine held the right arm with his left. His mother had always been direct in her orders and cruel in the manner she exacted punishment. Caine wanted vengeance against the Clovis Academy cadets, but he would wait for the plans of his parents. Even a sadist like Caine knew better than to cross Alfred and Magdalena Rosenburg. Caine always remembered his older brother Cush had tried to defy father. All of the children were forced to watch as father tortured and murdered Cush. The lesson was learned. Never cross father.

"What do you have in mind?" Alfred asked Magdalena.

"Caine is an idiot and should have his mind wiped. But I know you will never agree to do that to him so I propose we send in the professionals to clean this up. I am going to contact Ella and Ellis to eliminate those cadets."

Alfred nodded with a dour look on his face, "Do it. Kill them all."

Magdalena glared at Caine and his friends and licked her lips. "Killing them all is what I do best. Consider it done. I will bring in the Ragnarsson's to do the job. They never fail."

"Just make sure they kill them all!" Alfred growled as he stomped away from the scene, shoving Caine out of his way as he walked down the rear ramp of the ship. The cadets had killed

Daryl, his son, and they would all pay with their lives.

Magdalena licked her lips and felt no compassion for the cadets that were about to perish. Her only regret was that she would not be able to participate in the assassinations. She removed her holo-com device and began contacting the necessary individuals.

"No mercy for the dying," Magdalena said to herself. The saying was the Ragnarsson family motto and very appropriate in the current situation. The cadets would all die, there would be collateral deaths in the midst of the carnage, but in the end, the Rosenburg family and the Glorious Leader would escape the potential scandal as they had for the past two centuries. Magdalena wondered whether or not she had something wrong with her emotional upbringing due to her lack of empathy for those that were about to perish. She shrugged off her thoughts once one of the Ragnarsson assassins responded to her holo-com request. Within two days, the cadets would all be dead and the fickle public would forget all about the victims a week later.

The fact that the people cared little about their own freedoms made being evil easier for those like Magdalena. Little did she realize, her call to the Ragnarsson assassins was about to ignite a firestorm of public opinion that would result in an unintended consequence of all out civil war between the people of the eight solar systems

www.ingramcontent.com/pod-product-compliance
Lightning Source LLC
Chambersburg PA
CBHW070319190726
48291CB00014B/2354